THESE SCANDALOUS STREETS 3

THESE SCANDALOUS STREETS 3
Copyright © 2017 Tranay Adams. All rights reserved.

Warning: The unauthorized reproduction or distribution of this work is illegal. Criminal copyright infringement, including infringement without monetary gain, is investigated by FBI and is punishable by up to five (5) years in federal prison and a fine of $250,000.

All names, characters, and incidents depicted in this book are products of the author's imagination or are used fictitiously. Any resemblance to actual events, locales, organizations, or persons, living or dead, is entirely coincidental, and beyond the intent of the author and publisher.

No part of this book may be reproduced or transmitted in any form or by any means, electronic or mechanical, including photocopying, recording, or by any information storage and retrieval system, without permission in writing from the publisher.

These Scandalous Streets/ Tranay Adams-1st ed. © 2017

Cover Artist: Divine

PROLOGUE

It was dark outside, but it was beautiful, especially with half of the moon illuminating the night. It was the setting for lovers…two lovers to be exact.

"Who is this?"

Pain nodded his head to the astonishing voice coming through the speakers of his black on black '87 Cutlass Supreme with the original rims and tires. The loud music had that nigga's trunk rattling.

"Me."

Treasure gave him a smirk.

"Nah, seriously... Who is this?" he smiled.

"Me. I'm dead ass serious."

"For real?"

His eyebrows lifted in surprise, listening to one of the many unreleased songs that she had recorded.

"Uh huh."

She nodded rapidly, smiling now.

"Damnnnnnn."

He looked back and forth between her and the stereo broadcasting her song.

"Lil' mama, you can go. I'm impressed. I mean, I knew that you can sing, but not like this. This shit go."

He referred to the song, jabbing his finger at the stereo. She went to stop the music, but he playfully smacked her hand down, frowning.

"Fuck you doing?"

"I'm finna let you finish listening to what you were listening to beforehand."

"Nah, nah, we banging this 'til we see the crib."

He cranked up the volume on his stereo. Treasure threw her head back, laughing, and then she settled back in to the seat. Smiling, she interlocked her fingers with his and rode along, listening to the song that she recorded. Her eyes brought her back to Pain, and she swiftly pecked him on the cheek, bringing a smile to his face. They both nodded to her song, speeding through the streets. The city shown on his windshield and on the front passenger side window. Pain turned the music down, looking from his windshield to Treasure as he got closer to his house.

"I'ma just run in here and get this CD of this song I recorded. I'll be right back. Cool?"

He looked to her. She nodded yes. Pain pulled up across the street from his crib and killed the engine of his Cutlass. Having pulled the key out of the ignition, he opened the driver side door and stepped out into the street. He began whistling when he shut the door. It wasn't until he turned around that he found the shadows moving on the opposite side of the cars aligning his dimly lit block. He abruptly stopped whistling, and his brows wrinkled, wondering what the fuck it was that he was seeing. An alarm went off inside of his head, and he whipped around to get his gun which he had forgotten underneath the driver seat. That's when something bit him in the back of his leg, causing his face to ball up.

Pain grabbed the back of his leg and blood oozed from between his fingers, licking them wet. Turning around, he saw the hooded gunman pointing his banger at him. His eyelids snapped open, and he hobbled to the right, narrowly missing the bullet that shattered the driver's side window. Broken glass spilled and rained down onto the street, littering it. Still holding the back of his leg, he hobbled along as fast as he could.

He heard hurried footsteps that belonged to the gunman. He was moving all around him, taking shots. Some hit and some missed, but in the end, he was left bleeding and feeling light headed. Pain leaned down behind a car after taking one in the shoulder and his side. Gritting his teeth, he looked down to the ground and saw his blood pelting the surface. He felt like he was about to faint, so he had to get away before the nigga that was hunting him could put an end to his shit.

Right when he went to move, he felt something hot whizz through his calf. He howled in agony and fell on his stomach. He tried to push up off the surface, but something else hot entered his thigh. He grimaced and looked to where the shots had come from through narrowed eyelids. That's when he saw the hooded gunman pick himself up from the asphalt and run around the car, sneakers looking like flashes in the night. Seeing this made his heart pummel his chest bone. His adrenaline was pumping and the blood was rushing through his veins, fear shown in his eyes. He crawled away as fast as he could, but hearing the gunman on his ass, he knew that it was all over. He stopped where he was and looked up to see his predator's shadow eclipsing him on the ground. Two kicks to his side signaled for Pain to turn over on his back, and he did, wincing. He found himself staring up into the darkness beneath the hood. The hooded gunman snatched a rope chain with the continent of Africa on it from around his neck and stuffed it inside of the pocket of his hoodie. Afterwards, he took the time to observe his handiwork and lifted his gun, his glove finger curling around the trigger.

"Fuck away from my man!" a feminine voice ripped through the night's air.

Poc!

"Arrrrrrr!"

The hooded stranger propelled backwards, stumbling and falling on his back. He dropped his gun and it went spinning around in circles across the sidewalk, stopping at the edge of the curb. The weapon teetered like a see-saw. He scrambled to his feet, looking for his banger. He went to snatch it up with bullets flying all around him.

Poc!

"Bitch ass nigga!"

Poc!

"I'ma kill yo' mothafucking ass out here!"

Poc!

An angry Treasure approached the gunman with Pain's .45 automatic handgun, letting off shot after shot.

"Ugh!" the hooded shooter clenched his jaws tightly, feeling the impact of a second bullet. His hand was within an inch of picking up his burner when he felt something slam into his Kevlar bulletproof vest. He ran across the street, holding his chest and glancing over his shoulder, but that didn't stop Treasure's ass from taking shots at him, shattering the back window of parked cars and narrowly missing him. Treasure lowered her ratchet to her waistline and looked on as the gunman retreated. Once he was swallowed up by the darkness, she turned around to Pain. His face was twisted up in pain. He was bleeding from everywhere, kicking his right leg in agony.

"Oh my God."

Treasure dropped the .45 automatic and it hit the sidewalk. She sat on the ground and pulled her man into her lap, resting his head against her bosom. His eyelids were narrowed, and blood ran from the corners of his mouth, his head bobbling about.

"Stay awake, baby! Whatever you do, don't close your eyes. Keep them open," she said, looking down over his head, studying all of the holes in him. Her head shot up, and she looked around frantically, but there wasn't anyone in sight. Tears came running from her eyes and down her cheeks.

"Somebody help me! Help me, pleeeease!" Treasure's voice echoed throughout the night.

THESE SCANDALOUS STREETS 3

A Novel by Tranay Adams

CHAPTER ONE

The weather was quite nice that day. It was sunny with the occasional breeze. For as welcoming as it was that evening, an older man and his daughter were oblivious to it all. At the moment, they were at their loved one's grave stone, standing with their fingers interlocked with one another's. The daughter stood upright, holding a bouquet of roses while wetness slid down her cheeks. Her father took the time to pull out a folded handkerchief from his pocket and dab her face dry. His eyes bled his grief as well, but he knew at a time like this that he had to stay strong for the most important woman in his life now.

"You okay, baby girl?" Grief asked his child as he dried her cheeks. He looked sharp as fuck in his dark blue pinstriped suit and fedora. The black leather crocodile skin shoes, as well as their respective buckles were shining under the graces of the sun.

Treasure took the handkerchief from her father and began dabbing her own face dry.

"No, but I will be," she claimed in her white blouse with the ruffled collar which she wore underneath a grey vest and matching pencil skirt that hugged her curves. The material embraced her lower half like Saran Wrap.

No matter how many times they visited her grave, no matter how many times they saw her name and image on the black marble stone, their minds refused to accept the fact that Rose Jones, Treasure's mother and Grief's wife, was dead. Every time they came out to visit her, they hoped that it was a nightmare and that they'd both be awakened from their sleep somehow. Every time they visited, they ended up being disappointed, depressed, hurt, and in turmoil.

Treasure got down on her knees before her mother's grave and laid a bouquet of roses beside it. She then took the wine glass and the black bottle with the maroon label around the neck. Opening it, she poured the glass full and sat it on the other side of the grave stone, across from the flowers. Her father got down on his knees beside her and interlocked his fingers with hers. They stared down at the stone of the most wonderful woman either of them had known for a minute. Next, they hung their heads and shut their eyelids, saying a prayer that only they could hear. Once they'd finished, they got to their feet and met with Fat Rat and Buddah at the vehicle they'd been chauffeured in. Grief opened the back door of the car. He was just about to lead Treasure in when his left-hand spoke up.

"Fuck is he doin' here?"

Fat Rat tightened his jaws, and a vein bulged at his neck. Everyone else looked to see Pain standing at the hill. His eyes were focused down on them. There wasn't any doubt in Grief's mind that the young man had come to have a word with him. He couldn't help but admire his bravery, being that he threatened to have him killed if he ever saw him again.

"You want me and Buddah to wet his lil' young ass up, maine?" Fat Rat asked, trigger finger itching like he had poison ivy.

"Nah, I'd like to holla at him. Y'all two come with me."

He turned to Treasure.

"Baby girl, you stay here. I'll be right back."

She nodded, and he kissed her on the cheek. After motioning for his niggas to follow him, he fell in step to go holler at that nigga, Pain, to see where his head was.

****

Pain stood on one of the many hills of the cemetery with his thumbs hooked in the loops of his jeans. He wore a navy-blue bandana around his forehead, a matching thermal, and ACG Nike boots with the laces untied. It was hot out, but the occasional cool breeze would disturb the hairs of his thick, nappy beard. Behind him was an old-school Cutlass, sitting on those big chrome thangs. His right-hand man, Epic, played the front passenger seat while their home boy, Lil' Joe, sat in the backseat. At the moment, they were sharing a smoldering blunt between them, stinking up the interior of his ride. The two men looked to their home boy down to the people that he was focused on, who were a middle-aged man and a younger woman. They appeared to be standing over a grave stone, more than likely visiting a deceased loved one.

Pain had followed the middle-aged man and the younger woman, who were actually Grief and Treasure, to the cemetery. The thug was hoping to squash an old beef between himself and the OG. He came there looking for a peaceful conversation, but if he didn't get one…well, let's just say some real gangsta shit was going to happen on those resting grounds.

"Pain…Pain."

Hearing someone call his name, he slowly began to come back to the here and now.

"Huh?"

The husky man finally looked alive, turning toward the voice that was calling him. At the end of his line of vision, he found his home boy, Paco also known as Epic. His eyelids were narrowed into slits, and his eyes were red webbed. You could tell that his ass was high.

"Here, foolie."

Epic passed Pain the withering blunt, smoke wafting from it. When Pain took the blunt, he looked down and saw the ashes sprinkled over his shirt. He sighed and brushed the ashes off of his person, hoping that the small embers didn't burn any holes into his shirt.

Epic was a Haitian nigga of fair height and naturally curly hair. He had a cross inked between his eyes and two teardrops at the corner of his right eye. Located on his neck was a fading tattoo, Bullet Boy. Having lost both of his parents in a fire at the tender age of nine, he was sent to stay with his grandfather. It was there that he basically became the old man's slave, attending to his every beck and call. When he failed to complete the chores that he was assigned, or hadn't done them in the time frame he was given, he was beaten with a switch until he bled.

Living with his grandfather wasn't all that bad though. The old man taught him everything he knew about voodoo. It took some time, but Epic eventually got the hang of the practice. After his grandfather passed away from natural causes, Epic made the streets his home and ran the city with other misfits like himself. It was there that he eventually linked up with Lil' Joe, Pain, and his younger sister, Skylar. The three young men performed a blood brother ritual and promised to always stay down for one another.

"Damn, my nigga… Pain, you okay? Your head seems to be in another place," Lil' Joe said from the backseat, watching Pain take pulls from the blunt, letting a fog roll off of his tongue. He was a five-foot-seven cat of a brown hue. He had thick eyebrows and mustache. The nigga weighed a buck twenty-five soaking wet in boots.

Now, by no means was this little nigga giving it up in the streets like his homies, but don't get it fucked up. He would bust his gun, but that was only if his back was against the wall. Lil' Joe was the weakest in the trio's link, and they knew this. For a long time while they were juveniles running the streets, he wasn't accepted by them. He'd follow them around like a lost puppy, and occasionally be used as a punching bag whenever Epic was going through his shit. Every now and again, the fellas would throw him a little something from the licks they hit. When it became clear that the little mothafucka wasn't going anywhere no matter what was done to him, they finally accepted him into their little street family and put him down with the schemes they had planned. It wasn't long before Lil' Joe became as good as blood to them.

"I'm good," Pain replied, blowing smoke into the air and then passing the blunt back inside to Lil' Joe. When he finally turned around, he saw Grief and Treasure saying their final goodbyes to their loved ones whom he assumed was his ex's mother.

"Yo, Pain... how you want us to handle this, big dog?" Epic inquired, watching any and everything around him.

"Just play it cool," he replied.

"If old head on some bullshit, then we are taking it to the guns."

"I hear you, fam."

Epic took the bleezy from Lil' Joe and settled in the front seat.

"But what if the princess gets in the way?" he asked, referring to Treasure. Pain stared at Treasure. He didn't turn his head when he finally responded.

"No matter how it goes down, lil' mama walks. That's still my heart. A nigga can't live without that. As far as Grief and the rest of them OG niggas, they can get it."

"Straight like that," Epic said. Pain finally looked at his right-hand and said, "Straight like that."

He dapped both of his niggas up.

"Here them old niggas go now."

Epic spotted Grief and his niggas approaching. He mashed the blunt out in the ashtray, then he and Lil' Joe jumped out of the Cutlass. Wearing hard faces, they took their places on either side of Pain, hands lingering near the bulges on their waistlines. They didn't give a fuck about the influence that Grief held over the city. If he dared to harm one fucking hair on their home boy's head, then bullets were going to fly.

"Whoa, now."

Grief came up the hill holding up his hands in surrender. Fat Rat and Buddah were bringing up the rear.

"I came in peace, son. You can call off your dogs."

"I came in peace, too."

Pain gave Epic and Lil' Joe a nod, signaling to them that everything was okay. With that, his niggas dropped their hands to their sides, but they still stood by their nigga's side.

"What's the deal?" Pain asked, and he kept his scowling face as he threw his head back.

"Well, there was a time that we were like father and son. We looked at one another as family."

"Yeah, that was before you swore to have me killed," he reminded the OG.

"Only after you broke Treasure's heart," Fat Rat butted in their conversation. Him opening his mouth got hostile looks from Epic and Lil' Joe. Grief frowned and looked to his old friend. He turned to him and said something to him in a hushed tone, garnering a head nod from him. Home boy knew to stay in his place then. Grief turned back to Pain.

"Listen, son…uhhh, Trip. Can I call you, Trip?"

Pain shrugged and said, "It's on my birth certificate."

"Alright… Trip it is then."

He nodded.

"You gotta couple of ticks to spare, Trip?"

Pain took a deep breath and shut his eyelids briefly, slowly nodding his head. Grief turned to his niggas and told them to stay where they were so that he could holler at the young man in private. Having left his men orders, the OG motioned for Pain to follow him. The two of them walked across the cemetery. Grief held his wrist behind his back, and Pain kept his hands inside of his pockets as they strolled along. He couldn't help but wonder what the old man had to say to him. The last time they chopped it up, they swore that if they saw one another again that there was going to be gun smoke. Although it was all said out of anger, they both took what was said between one another very seriously.

"So what's up, Bernard?" Pain addressed him by his government name. Grief looked to the young man with furrowed brows.

"Bernard, huh? I guess that's just where we're at with it."

Pain continued to look ahead, wearing a straight face. The OG cleared his throat with a fist to his mouth.

"Do you still love my daughter?"

"A lil' bit."

"A lil' bit my ass, Trip. You know besides Treasure's own security, I have a couple of my guys follow her just as a precaution. There have been many occasions that they'll spot you lurking there in the shadows. The first time, they were going to blow you away, but I gave them orders to fallback. I figured then that if you loved my baby girl like I love my Rose, then the two of you should be together, regardless of what anybody has to say, ya hear me?"

"Yeah, I hear you," he stopped and faced him.

"And I do love her. I want her like I want my next breath."

"Well, then you're gonna have to prove it. I can tell you now that it's not gonna be easy to win my baby girl over."

"I can see that. A nigga been busting his ass try'na get her back, for real, for real, but she ain't try'na fuck with me," he told him straight up.

"She won't accept my calls, text, or none of that shit. I popped up at the house to see her, and she curved my ass. I'm all outta ideas now. I don't know what to do, and truthfully…" he looked around to make sure no one was watching them and saw his niggas as well as Grief's eyes on them.

"… I'm scared. I'm scared shitless."

"Scared?"

Grief's forehead ran with lines. He placed his hand on Pain's shoulder.

"Scared of what?"

Pain fidgeted with his fingers for a minute, and then looked up at him with glassy eyes.

"I'm scared of losing the love of my life."

Pain blinked his eyelids and swallowed the ball of nervousness in his throat.

"I'm absolutely terrified that's she's gone out of my life, and there's nothing I can ever do to get her back."

He looked down and continued to fidget with his fingers.

"Look at me, son," Grief said as he gripped both of Pain's shoulders and pressed his thumbs against his neck, trying to get him to look him in the eyes.

"Look at me."

Reluctantly, Pain looked up at him, tears threatening to slide down his cheeks.

"You still gotta chance. My baby girl is still in love with chu. She's just hurt. That's all. She's hurting real bad."

He shut his eyelids briefly and took a deep breath.

"If you want her back, then you're gonna have to start trying hard… real hard."

"What do I do?"

"That I do not know," he admitted.

"But I'll tell you this… if you want something bad enough, then you'll be willing to do any and everything in your power to obtain it. There is no such thing as 'sky's the limit' when it comes down to love. You hear me?"

Grief tilted his head down and looked up at the thug.

"There is no such thing as 'sky's the limit' when it comes down to love. You got that?"

Pain nodded and wiped away the tears that trickled from his eyes.

"Good. Now, gimme some."

He opened his arms, and Pain embraced him. The OG kissed him on the side of the face and embraced him tighter, patting him on the back.

"I love you, son."

"I love you too, pop."

He patted his back. They broke their embrace, and Grief patted him on his shoulder. He then gave him a nod and retreated back to his men. Pain watched the old heads board the limousine, leaving the chauffeur holding up the back door for Treasure. Oddly enough, she was standing beside the limousine and staring up at Pain, eyes lingering on him. At that precise moment, tears slowly descended down their cheeks, looking like small crystals below the sunlight. The staring seemed to have lasted a century, until Treasure slipped on her shades. Pain stood there until the limousine had vanished. Afterwards, he retreated back to his Cutlass where his home boys were. Epic and Lil' Joe embraced him in a group hug. Right after, they got back inside of the hood classic and took their leave.

CHAPTER TWO

Treasure sat in the backseat of the chauffeur driven vehicle, wiping her crying eyes with a balled-up Kleenex. Once she was done, she lowered her black sunglasses back on her face. At that moment, Grief opened the backdoor and whipped his ratchet out so that it wouldn't be stabbing him in his hip once he sat down. Sliding inside on the butter soft leather seats, he shut the door behind him and stashed his banger inside of a secret stash space. He threw his hand over the top of the seat and looked to his daughter. From the look on her face, he could tell that she had still been crying which meant that she was still grieving over the loss of her mother.

"You gonna be all right, baby girl?" he asked, rubbing the back of her neck.

"I'll be okay, dad."

She sniffled and wiped her red nose.

"You know I love you more than anything in this world, right?"

"Uh, huh," she nodded, fidgeting with the ball of Kleenex. Grief leaned over and kissed her on the cheek.

"Now, let cho old man see that smile I love so much."

Treasure gave her father a halfhearted smile. It wasn't what he was used to getting, but he'd accept it. Grief smiled at his daughter and patted her on the knee.

"That's my sweet pea."

The OG pulled a cigar from inside of his suit and fired it up, blowing smoke into the air. He fanned the cloud of smoke with his jeweled hand and cracked the window just enough to let the smoke out.

"What are your plans for the rest of the day?"

"I gotta hit the studio to begin recording for this album," she told him.

"How about chu?" she asked and looked to him, waiting for his answer.

"Ummm… uh."

He took the cigar from out of his mouth and brushed the imaginary lint from off of his suit as he cleared his throat, holding his fist to it.

"Awww, dad."

Treasure threw her head back, sounding disappointed. She brought her head back down and grasped her father's hand. This was the same hand that his gold wedding ring was on. It gleamed underneath the rays of the sun. When he looked to it, the memory of him and his late wife standing before one another saying their wedding vows flashed across his mind.

"What?"

He looked to her, acting like he didn't have a clue about what she was talking about.

"You're going to stay up all day and night trying to solve mom's murder, aren't you?"

Grief took a deep breath and tapped his cigar, dumping ashes into an ashtray.

"Yes I am... I've grown obsessed with finding out who murdered her, and I'll never know a moment's rest until I know who did it."

Treasure focused her attention out of the tinted window, blowing hot air and causing her shoulders to slump.

"The police have already closed the case. You know that after forty-eight hours the window for finding the suspect gets smaller and smaller. Well, it's been two years now. I know them crackas ain't thinking about solving your mother's murder, but I am, and when I find the son of a bitch that did that to her…"

He stared off into space, sloping his eyebrows and scrunching his nose. He clenched his jaws so mothafucking tight that they pulsated. Tears danced at the corners of his eyes, and he squeezed his cigar so tight that the ashes oozed out of it. The ashes trickled down to the floor, landing on the tip of his designer shoe. Seeing her father lost in his rage, worriment went across Treasure's face, and she gripped his hand, calling his name over and over again.

"Dad… dad… dad!"

"Huh?"

He blinked his eyelids repeatedly and looked around all wide eyed and shit. It was as if he didn't know where he was.

"Are you…are you okay?" she asked, concerned, cupping his face and turning him toward her. He nodded yes and looked at his hand. The ruined cigar was still wedged between his fingers. He looked to his foot, and ashes were lying on top of it.

"Yeah… yeah, I'm fine."

He nodded and let the window down, tossing the ruined cigar out of it. It hit the street while the car was in motion, tumbling and sending embers flying down the road. Once he let the window back up, he turned to his daughter.

"I'm sorry. I hope I didn't scare you, baby girl. I just became so angry that I lost it there, you know?"

He patted the hand that she had on his knee, lovingly.

"Yeah... I know, dad. I'm sorry if I seemed bothered by you staying up all of the time, studying that footage. It's just that you hardly ever sleep these days, and you need your rest. You being up for days at a time isn't good for your heart. I already lost one parent. I'm not trying to lose another."

Grief looked to his daughter, and tears had accumulated in her eyes. He could tell by the way that she was looking that she was terrified of losing him like she'd lost her mother. He was pretty sure that she'd fall apart if something were to happen to him. Although he wanted to find Rose's murderer and put a bullet in his head, he didn't want to fuck around and lose his daughter in the process. Her life mattered more to him than making his wife's murderer pay for his sins, but letting it go had proven to be harder than he imagined, so until he had caught up with the nigga and laid him out, he was going to keep on hunting him. If he had to, he'd chase his bitch ass to the ends of the earth.

"I know you worry about me, baby girl. But I'll never get any sleep as long as I know that your mother's murderer is out there still roaming the streets like shit is sweet. The son of a bitch is gonna realize he made a grave mistake the night he broke into our home, and your daddy is going to see to it."

Treasure took a deep breath and laid her head against her father's shoulder. Staring ahead, she began talking to him.

"If this is what you have to do to find your peace, then keep on keeping on."

"Thanks, baby girl."

He patted her hand which was on his arm and kissed the top of her head.

"I assure you... once I find this cock sucka, it will bring the both of us closure."

"It most definitely will, dad. It most definitely will." Treasure squeezed her father's hand affectionately and then kissed him on the cheek. She then focused her attention out of the tinted window, thinking back to when she saw Pain at the cemetery. It had been a few months since she'd last seen him, and even with all that had happened, she missed the hell out of him. She hated herself for feeling the way she did, but she couldn't help herself. Her heart yearned for him. It wanted him bad, but her mind told her it was best that she stayed away from him.

Treasure thought back to the day Pain put hands on a nigga that had disrespected her. She'd never forget that day. She would remember it like she remembered the date of her birth.

It was ninety degrees, and the sun was shining. All that could be heard were the hoots and hollers of men and women along with the roaring of engines from the cars and motorcycles. The block party was as live as a Beyoncé concert. The women were out in skimpy clothing while the fellas were out in their best clothes and jewelry. D-boys and ballers alike were out bragging, boasting, and shooting their mack at everything with big tits and a fat ass.

There was drinking and smoking, along with a lot of talking and laughter. Tricked out vehicles, four wheelers, and motorcycles made their way down the street like it was a mothafucking parade going on. Niggas and bitches were ghost riding whips and doing dangerous stunts on their bikes, putting on one hell of a show for the onlookers.

Everyone was having themselves a good old time, especially Treasure and her home girl, Skylar.

"So... who you got cho eye on, boo?" *Treasure asked Skylar as she sucked on a strawberry Tootsie Roll sucker. Her eyes were hidden behind oversized designer shades. She was in a hot pink bikini top and camouflage cargo pants that were cut to look like Daisy Dukes.*

"Bitch, you betta act like you know. I been scoping out that short buff ass nigga, Tank," *she claimed, staring down the block at a little muscular nigga wearing a motorcycle helmet and black tank top. He wore jean shorts and Air Force Ones that were a little scuffed up due to riding his bike most of that day. Surrounding him were a couple of his home boys who were either polishing their bikes or inspecting them. All of the men were talking among themselves no matter what activity they were engaged in.*

"You always did love them lil' niggas. I ain't mad at chu though. Gone, girl," *she replied as she cracked a smile at her best friend. Her girl, Skylar, was dressed in a white bikini top and matching capri pants. Her blonde hair was braided into cornrows.*

"You sleeping, sis. Them lil' niggas be having big wallets and big dicks."

She tilted her sunglasses down and gave her a look that she read 'you ain't feeling me though'. Treasure took the sucker out of her mouth and bent at the waist laughing.

"Sky, you know your ass is too much for me."

"I'm speaking the truth. I'll swear on a stack of Bibles."

Skylar held up her right hand to God.

"I believe you. My bitch ain't never gotta lie."

"Fucking right."

They gave one another a high five.
"I'm hungry as a hostage. What about chu?"
"Shit, I could eat."
"Hold up."
Skylar cupped her hand around her mouth and yelled across the street to a tall cat in a backwards baseball cap and apron that read 'Kiss the cook.'
"Yo, Kerwin! Hook me and my girl up with some plates!"
"Fuck I look like... Florence out this mothafucka?"
He took the time to wipe his sweaty face and forehead with a rag before flipping over a few hamburger patties.
"You betta get cho itty bitty ass over here and make you a plate," he said to her as he stuffed the rag into his back pocket. He didn't even bother to look in her direction.
"As fine as I am? You want me to fix my own plate?"
"You goddamn right."
He nodded, taking the time out to take a swig from his flask.
"As fine as yo' ass is, and you ain't coming off no pussy, ya dick tease. You betta get over here and help yo'self."
Skylar blew hot air and rolled her eyes, turning back around to her girl, Treasure.
"I'm finna get us a plate."
"All right, girl. See if they got any bread pudding left."
"All right. I'll be right back."
She dapped her up and went on about her business. Treasure smirked, seeing her home girl sashay across the street, her hips swinging her cute little bubble butt from

side to side. She shook her head and giggled, thinking of how much of a trip she was. Little mama could make her laugh by just being herself. It was one of the few things that she loved about her.

"Yo, Treaaaasurrrreee!"

"Fuck! Here this nigga come," Treasure said under her breath, hating to be called. She didn't even have to turn around to see who it was. She already knew that it was that fool ass nigga, Chauncey. He'd been on her like stink on shit ever since she and Skylar pulled up. Although Treasure curved his ass repeatedly, the persistent mothafucka wouldn't take no for an answer, thinking that she was just playing hard to get.

"Yo, Treas'," the six-foot-four, milk dud head dude called after her, bobbing his way in her direction. He wore a white washcloth on top of his dome and a wife beater which was stained with sweat around the collar and armpit. His entire form was shiny from sweat. His black ass looked like he was about to melt under that hot ass sun.

Treasure rolled her eyes and shook her head. She was tired of being nice to this mothafucka, trying to keep shit calm and peaceful, because she didn't want to fuck up the function for everyone else.

"I'm tired of this thirsty ass nigga. Nigga can't take no for an answer or somethin'... damn."

Before Treasure knew it, Chauncey was grabbing her by her arm, roughly.

"Yo, Treasure. I know you heard—"

He was cut short by her snatching her arm away from his grasp.

"Don't touch me," she said as she balled up her face spitefully.

"Fuck you mean, don't touch you?" he scowled, talking through his big ass chapped lips and showcasing his chipped front tooth.

"Who the hell you think you are, witcho fake boujee ass?"

"Oh, now I'm boujee 'cause I don't wanna talk to yo' old ugly ass?"

This brought laughter from every direction which caused Chauncey's head to take in the full scope of his surroundings. He and Treasure had stolen damn near everyone at the block party's attention. A lot of eyes were on them.

"Nigga, get off of my dick! I tried to be nice about it, but apparently, you do not comprehend it, so allow me to break it down for yo' dumb ass," she said as she placed her manicured hand on her hip and switched the weight of her body to her other low top All Star Chuck Taylor Converse.

"I'm not fucking witchu, boo boo. You aren't my type, so please... please leave me the fuck alone."

She moved her neck like ghetto girls did when they were popping that shit at a nigga. This drew more laughter and niggas egging on the situation.

"Awww, hell nah! Chauncey... my nigga, I know you ain't 'bout to let home girl play you out like that," one of the bystanders said from the sidelines.

"Prison done made the homie soft now. The Chauncey I know would've been smacked fire from that hoe!" another bystander spoke. Chauncey looked all around at everybody laughing and egging the situation on. Feeling embarrassed, he turned beet red in the face and then scowled. His top lip trembled like he was an angry wolf ready to attack.

"Get cho hands off my bitch, nigga!" Skylar called out from across the street. When Treasure glanced in her direction, she was pulling a big ass butcher's knife from out of a slab of ribs and running toward her. Although Skylar was about hundred and thirty pounds soaking wet, she would bring it to anyone behind her loved ones, straight up.

"Fuck you think you talking to?" Chauncey barked, spittle flying off his lips. Treasure looked him up and down like he wasn't shit.

"Yo' mothafucking ass!" she spat without fear, knowing damn well that he could squash her like a cockroach, but she refused to back down.

"I swear on my Uncle Bernie, Chauncey... If you touch my bestie, I'ma kill yo' punk ass!" Skylar swore, running as fast as she could to Treasure's defense. People were moving out of her way, and some of them were even looking at her like she was crazy. They couldn't wait to see how everything was going to play out.

"Bitch, chu got me fucked up!"

Chauncey glared at Treasure and brought his hand around his back. He was about to smack flames out of that ass. He swung his hand from around his back, cutting through the air as it headed toward Treasure's face. She squeezed her eyelids shut and waited for the impact of his palm.

Pat!

Treasure peeled her eyelids open one at a time. A surprised look came across her face when she saw Pain twisting Chauncey's arm behind his back and kicking him in the back of his knee. The impact dropped his big ass down to one knee. He wore a mask of hurt as he clenched his jaws tightly, bone structure appearing and disappearing.

"Now, I know I didn't just see you raise your hand to a woman, did I?"

Pain's eyebrows arched, and his nose scrunched up.

"Naahhh," Chauncey said in pain, his face registering his hurt.

"I raised my hand to a bitch. Arrrgh!" he hollered out, wrist bone crackling when Pain twisted it.

"Apologize to the lady!"

Pain glared down at him. He was about ready to break his fucking wrist for being so mothafucking smart at the mouth.

"You okay, Treas'?"

Skylar approached her brother and best friend. That big ass butcher's knife was still in her fist.

"Yeah," she nodded, having given her a hug.

"Thanks to yo' brother."

She looked at Pain and he presented her with a smile and a blink of his eyelid. The block party was focused on all of them now.

"Now, like I was saying, apologize to the lady," Pain gritted at Chauncey.

"My homie ain't gotta apologize fa shit!" a voice rang from their right. When they looked, there was a dude about five foot eight and another about five foot six. They were rocking hard faces and tank tops, being that it was hot outside. In their fists were knives that looked like they had been crafted in prison. The fingerprint smudged blades twinkled under the sunlight.

"Fuck if he don't," another voice rang out from the left. When everyone looked, Epic and Lil' Joe were standing there with their bangers pointed at the niggas that posed as threats to their home boys.

"You stupid mothafuckas brought knives to a gunfight."

Lil' Joe shook his head like to say 'you stupid ass niggas'. Seeing the guns, the fools that were ready to ride out on Pain just a minute ago dropped their knives. They clasped to the ground one after another.

"Now, apologize to my home girl," Pain pressed him. In his mind, he was daring him to go against the grain so that he could fuck his shit up.

"Hold up. Matter of fact, I want chu to say this to her."

He leaned closer to his ear and whispered.

"What? I ain't 'bout to say that shit."

He stared at him angrily through the corner of his eye. In a flash, Pain's .45 automatic handgun was off of his waistline and being pressed to the side of that nigga, Chauncey's, melon.

"I'm not gone tell yo' bitch ass again, nigga."

"Man, just tell her what he told you to so that we can go," the five-foot-eight nigga urged his homie. With pain in his face, Chauncey brought his trembling head up and looked up at Treasure.

"I apologize from the bottom of my heart, beautiful black queen. Please excuse my idiocy, but sometimes niggas lose all decency when in the presence of such a phenomenal woman."

With the apology given, Pain looked to Treasure to see if she was pleased. She smiled and gave him a nod.

"Apology accepted," she told Chauncey's punk ass. Pain released Chauncey's wrist, and he rose to his feet, wincing and rubbing it. His home boys grabbed one of his arms each and made to leave, but Pain calling them back froze them in their tracks.

"Where y'all going?" Pain asked with furrowed brows, ratchet at his side.

"We bouta breeze," the five-foot-eight nigga told him.

"No, y'all not. Ain't no hard feelings. Yo, man just got outta line, and I had to put his big ass in check. This is me and my niggas' shindig. Y'all niggas help y'all selves to some BBQ and something to drink. You're more than welcome."

They all exchanged glances.

"I'm not asking you. I'm telling you," he demanded, putting his foot down. Seeing that the young thug wasn't bullshitting with their asses, Chauncey's home boys walked him toward the tall nigga manning the grill.

"Yo, OG," Pain called out across the street to Kerwin.

"Hook these fine gentlemen up with something to eat and drink... oh, and some of that loud, too. We still got that on deck, right?"

"Fa sho'," Kerwin nodded.

"I'll take care of 'em."

"That's love."

He pounded his fist against his chest and his old head pounded his fist against his own. Afterwards, he tucked his steel on his waistline and addressed the people at the block party. They were still eyeballing him.

"What y'all looking at? The party ain't over. Cut the music back on, and let's keep this bitch jumping."

With that said, the music cut back on, four wheelers and motorcycles were revved back up, and the tricked-out car continued to stunt out in the middle of the street.
"Bro, you good?"
Skylar hugged Pain, wrapping both of her arms around her brother.
"I'm always good, Bird," he called her by her childhood nickname. She'd gotten the name due to her chicken legs.
"How about chu, ma?"
A grinning Pain threw his head back.
"I'm fine, thanks to you."
Treasure smiled and batted her eyelashes, openly flirting with him. She always had a thing for big niggas, and Pain's fine ass was one with swag. On top of that, he was funny, affectionate, aggressive, and thug as shit. Homie was definitely her cup of tea. The only way she stayed away from him was because she didn't know how her girl, Skylar, would feel about her fucking with her brother. She had to have her blessing before she decided to give him a shot.
"Ahem."
Epic cleared his throat with a fist to his mouth, wanting her to mention him and his little nigga. He had just finished tucking his twin nine-millimeters on his waistline. Treasure looked to him and Lil' Joe, smiling.
"My bad. Thanks to you, Epic, and Lil' Joe."
"Don't mention it, lil' mama. That wasn't 'bout nothing. Come on, Lil' Joe."
Epic tapped his little nigga's chest, and they walked off to get back up with the chicks they were chopping it up with before the beef popped off.

Treasure and Pain stood where they were, smiling at one another. It became apparent to Skylar that they were feeling one another. She discovered this when looking back and forth between them. Seeing this caused Skylar to smile as well. She always knew that her best friend and only brother had a thing for one another. The only reason why she didn't push them to go the distance was because she didn't want to be the one to blame if things went sour, but here they were now, and it appeared as if that situation earlier could manifest into a beautiful relationship.

"Well, ummm... I'll go get us those plates, hooker. You want something, bro?" Skylar asked her sibling.

"A Corona is always good," he said as his smile stretched further across his face while he held both of Treasure's hands in his own, staring into her eyes. He licked his lips on some LL Cool J shit. He never took his eyes off the aspiring songstress as he kissed her delicate hands.

"Sky," Treasure called for her bestie's attention. She gave her a look that asked for her approval to take things further with her brother. In return, she got a head nod that let her know that everything was okay.

"I'ma leave you guys be then."

Skylar smiled and rubbed her girl's shoulder. She walked back toward the house so she could make her and Treasure's plates.

From that day forward, Treasure and Pain were inseparable. The only time that they weren't together was when Pain was in the streets making moves. After two months, they became an item, and everybody in the hood celebrated their union. When Grief caught wind of his baby girl seeing some trap nigga, he called for a car to pick him up and they had a long talk. He laid down the law on how he wanted his little princess to be treated, and should she be made to feel anything less than royalty while she was with him, then there was going to be hell to pay.

Grief and Pain developed a father and son bond over the next two years. In fact, the OG had so much love for him that he cut him a sweet deal on some bricks that he had on deck. Pain fucked up when he smashed Treasure's cousin, Fiona. Grief wanted to put the guns to him, but his baby girl pleaded with him to let him breathe. Putting aside his ego, Grief allowed Pain to keep his life, but he still had to punish him for the violation, so he cut him off of his drug supply. This left Pain and his crew hurt. They had no choice but to find another plug, and they did. The price was a little higher than what they were used to, but the work was supreme.

Grief grasped his daughter's leg, and she looked at him. He told her that she was home and nodded to her baby mansion. She grabbed her purse and kissed her father goodbye, telling him that she loved him. They parted with her promising to call him later to check on him. For now, she was going to pour herself up a glass of wine and enjoy a hot bubble bath before she hit the studio that night.

CHAPTER THREE

Pain, Epic and Lil' Joe retreated to the Chevy and hopped in, slamming the doors shut one after another. Epic fired up the vehicle and drove off, traveling down the road of the cemetery. With a fixed frown on his face, Lil' Joe stared out of the back window, looking at all of tombstones that they sped past. He observed the scenery as Epic and Pain chopped it up among themselves.

"So does the OG want war or peace?" Epic asked.

"No doubt."

"Good. We weren't try'na let no bullshit get in the way of us gettin' this money."

"You damn right."

"So what's up next on the itinerary?" Lil' Joe asked no one in particular from the backseat.

"Shit, besides us seeing the plug tonight, the agenda is clear 'til 8:00."

"Cool."

Lil' Joe rubbed his jeweled hands together and licked his lips.

"I'm try'na hit up the strip club."

"Yo, I forgot to tell y'all niggas that I'm 'pose to have dinner tonight with baby sis, so I'ma have to take a rain check on this one. Y'all got it covered though, right?"

He looked from Epic to Lil' Joe.

"Yeah, we got it," Lil' Joe answered. Epic nodded and said, "We got it faded."

"My niggas."

Pain grinned, dapping up his niggas.

"Alright, they'll be closing in..." Lil' Joe's voice got quieter as he glanced at his watch, trying to estimate when they were making a move. He was a year younger than Pain and Epic which would make him thirteen years old. That night, he was dressed down in black and rocking gloves like the rest of them. He was sitting behind the wheel of an old Cadillac Seville, playing the getaway driver. In fact, the little nigga was the driver on all their licks. He was good at his job... really good.

"... fifteen minutes. I'ma keep this big mothafucka running. Y'all niggas run in there, handle y'all business, and get the fuck out."

"No doubt," a young Pain replied.

"You ready, my nigga?"

He looked at his right-hand man through the rearview, who was in the backseat.

"I was born ready, dog," a young Epic responded, pulling a black bandana over the lower half of his face and cocking his nine-millimeter Beretta. His face was a mask of seriousness and determination.

"Trip, are you sure about this?" a younger Skylar asked. She was the only one out of all of them that wasn't dressed up for the mission that night. Nah, she was dressed up like any other little girl, except her hair was done in afro puffs on either side. Pain looked into the backseat and saw the glassy, puppy dog eyes on his little sister. Before he knew it, tears were sliding down her face. Reaching into the backseat, he wiped away her tears with his thumb.

"Yeah, I'm positive," he assured her.

"This is how we eat, and from the sound of that stomach of yours, you're past due for some grub. Hell, we all are for that matter."

Pain had been hearing all of their stomachs grumbling that night, his own included. He knew that something had to be done, and something had to be down now. He had vowed to his sister when they broke out of foster care that he was going to take care of her no matter what, and there wasn't any way he wasn't keeping his word.

"I'm...I'm scared, Trip. I gotta bad feeling about all of this. Let's just go home," she cried, tears accumulating in her eyes and threatening to fall. Just then, she broke down sobbing, and he reached over into the backseat, hugging her lovingly. As her form shook in his arms, he kissed her on the side of the head and promised her that they were going to be in and out, and once they were finished, they all were heading over to McDonalds to eat. He'd planned on ordering her any and everything that she wanted. That would be her reward for staying strong while he went to handle his business.

Epic looked at the exchange between the two of them and felt her pain. He knew that his ace was the only family that she had out on the street. He even thought about talking Pain into falling back and letting him and Lil' Joe handle things, but he knew that the stubborn bastard wasn't going to allow that to happen.

"I love you," Pain told his sister after breaking their embrace.

"I love you, too," she whimpered and wiped her eyes with a curled finger.

"All right then, L.J. Hold it down."

He dapped him up. As he was doing this, Epic was pulling a black bandana over the lower half of his face and sliding black sunglasses on afterwards. He cocked the slide on his nine-millimeter Beretta and said to Pain, "Come on, nigga."

Pain and Epic hopped out of the G-ride and ran into the liquor store. Entering, they found the Arabic store clerk mopping the floor and humming to the foreign music coming from the little boom-box on the counter. When he saw the two gunmen, his eyes bugged, and he dropped the mop, freezing with fear.

"Who else is in here?" Epic asked, his gun-hand extended as he approached the clerk. The frightened man tried to say something, but his mouth couldn't form the words, so Epic gave him some incentive by smacking him across the head with his nine-millimeter, opening a nasty gash. He stumbled backwards but caught his balance by grabbing a hold of the counter.

"Don't make me ask you again!" the juvenile barked.

"No one...I'm here alone," the clerk said, touching his head and coming away with blood. Pain watched the door while his home boy handled his business. He looked on, admiring his nigga's gangsta. His demeanor reminded him of O-Dog in Menace II Society.

Epic grabbed his victim by the collar and ushered him through the door, behind the bulletproof glass of the counter. He brought him to the cash register and said, "Open up the drawer, 'fore I open ya fuckin' chest!"

The clerk did as he was instructed. The drawer of the register chimed open, and the clerk emptied its contents into a brown paper bag. Once he was done, Epic relieved him of his wallet and tossed it into the bag as well. He snatched the bag from the clerk, rolled it up, and tossed it over to his right-hand man.

"Aye, grab a bottle of that Hen Dawg," Pain said, stuffing the brown paper bag into his jeans. Reaching for the bottle of Hennessy on the shelf, Epic caught the clerk reaching for something stashed behind the counter. He jabbed him in the mouth with his gun, busting his lips. The nigga stumbled backwards and fell on his back, holding his bleeding grill.

Epic tucked his ratchet into the small of his back and christened his victim with a merciless beating, lumping homie up something awful. The thrashing was so brutal that Pain cringed and turned his head. Epic stomped and kicked the clerk for all of five minutes. Once he was done, his sneakers and pants legs were spotted with specks of blood. The clerk lay on the floor with a bloody face, groaning in pain. Epic spat on him, grabbed the bottle of Hennessy, and fled from the store with his brother. Pain was right behind his homie as they ran out of the store, running as hard as he could, breathing huskily.

Epic and Pain's eyes were set on the getaway car. Lil' Joe had it running. They could see smoke wafting from its exhaust pipe. Skylar was in the backseat with her face pressed against the window. She smiled seeing her brother and his home boy running in her direction. Pain smiled behind the bandana as well, but that jovial expression disappeared when he saw a police car headed for them, coming in the opposite direction. His heart pounded inside of his chest, sounding like a cannon on a pirate ship going off, back to back.

"Oh shit!" Pain's eyes lit up. Hearing him, Epic glanced over his shoulder but kept on going.

"What?"

"The rollers, my nigga. We can't get in the car. If we get knocked, they'll snatch up sis and Lil' Joe, and put them in a home."

Epic and Pain turned around running in the direction that they'd come from. Skylar was in the backseat window crying and screaming, fogging up the glass as she pounded her fist against it. The police car got as close as it could to the fleeing suspects before coming to a stop. Its doors flew open, and two white niggas in uniforms hopped out, pursuing them. They may have been close, but the youths were fast... real fast. They widened the distance between them and ducked off inside of an alley.

"Yo, I ain't try'na see the inside of no cell, dog! I'm finna bang it out with them boys."

Epic presented Pain his thoughts, hoisting his gun up at his shoulders.

"Nigga, fuck no! You kill one of them crackas, and they gone gas our black asses for sho'. We'll take our chances on foot. Let's split up at the end of this alley."

He nodded toward the end of the alley.

"Okay?"

Epic nodded.

"Alright. Toss the burners."

They tossed their guns and glanced over their shoulders. The police were still on their asses.

"You go left, and I'll go right. We'll click back up on the block."

"Okay."

"Got chu."

Epic nodded, running against the wind, ruffling his clothing.

"I love you, E," he replied, his clothing ruffling as he ran against the wind.

"I love you too. See you on the block," he said, seeing the end of the alley coming up ahead. The young niggas split, meeting the end of the alley, going their respective ways. The police went right, the same way that Pain went, leaving Epic a free man.

Pain found himself slowing down, having gotten exhausted. He knew he had to find some place to hide, or that was his ass when the cops caught up to him. Seeing another alley, he ran inside and discovered a trash bin. Lifting the lid, he climbed inside and quietly shut it. The police came to a stop on the sidewalk, breathing heavily and looking around. They didn't know where their suspect had disappeared to, but they were determined to find him. Hearing a lone can fall from a big ass rat darting from its hiding place drew their attention to an alley. One of the police men smiled fiendishly and tapped his partner, pointing to the trash bin he believed their suspect had hid inside. They took one step forward, and heard a window imploding, glass shards raining down in the street. Right after the glass shattering came the car alarm. Their heads snapped in the direction that the noise came from. They took off running in the direction where they heard the noise. Ahead, Epic stepped out with an old rusted pipe in his hand, talking big shit.

"Ol' pussy ass cops... Y'all white niggas can't catch me!" he called out from where he stood. He waited until they'd gotten close enough and then launched the pipe at one of them, striking him in the eye and taking him out of the chase. Epic then took off. The lone cop on his ass dove forward and tackled him to the street. The cop got on his feet and drew his nightstick, taking it to Epic's ass. The young nigga blocked the lethal strike of the rod with his limbs as best he could, but when the cop's partner joined the fight, he didn't stand a chance. Having beaten the living shit out of Epic, the cops holstered their nightsticks and cuffed him, pulling him to his wobbly legs. Blood in his right eye, he squeezed it shut and looked around through his good eye. He saw Pain darting across the street. Once he'd reached the opposite end, he held his gaze and then tapped his fist against his chest. Pain gave him a nod before the police ushered him away.

Epic did four years in juvenile hall for the crimes that he committed. He took his charge on the chin like a mothafucking man and never uttered his home boy's name. When he came home, that nigga Pain made sure he was straight. Afterwards, they got back to what they did the best...hustling.

When Epic pulled up in front of Pain's house, he killed the engine and tossed him the keys. Everyone got out and assembled on the sidewalk. They dapped one another up and went their separate ways. Pain went to relax a little before he had to meet up with his sister that night for dinner. Epic and Lil' Joe sped off to hit up the strip club and then later to meet up with the plug.

CHAPTER FOUR

The sun was just setting when Grief had finally made it home. As soon as he opened his front door, he carried his short form over to the mini-bar and poured himself up a glass of Jack Daniels. After swirling the ice around inside of the glass, he took a sip of it and hissed as the spicy liquor met with his taste buds. Licking his lips, he took another sip and made his way down the corridor of his house, stopping at the door of his study. Turning the doorknob, Grief pushed his way inside of the room and sat down at his executive chair. It was there that he spotted the portrait of his gorgeous wife. He picked up the portrait and brought it closer to him, resting it on his stomach. He continued to take casual sips from his glass, finding his eyes stinging and then tears streaming down his cheeks. She had been dead a year now, and each day, he grew to love and miss her that much more. At times, he found his heart hurting with great emotional pain, and he wished that he could stop it. There was a big empty space in him, and he knew that it would never close until he was reunited with the love of his life.

Grief swirled the alcohol around inside of his glass, thinking back to how he'd first decided to make an honest woman out of his wife.

Grief had met Rose twenty-three years ago. It was love at first sight for the both of them, but their union was forbidden. See, at the time, the OG was the lieutenant to a very powerful drug lord by the name of Khaza. Khaza was a psychopath and felt all women were inferior to him since he was a man. Unfortunately, this asshole was Rose's husband. She thought she was dealing with Dr. Jekyll and Mr. Hyde the way he teetered between the man she'd fallen in love with and the monster she was living with. In the beginning, he was funny, charming and as sweet as apple pie, but a year into their marriage, everything changed.

Khaza had become physically and mentally abusive. He beat her ass for breakfast, lunch, dinner, and a midnight snack. He made his wife his very own maid and sex slave, making her participate in despicable acts that would haunt her in her sleep. The son of a bitch thought he could make up for the things that he did to her by buying her flowers, candy, jewelry, and other expensive gifts, but absolutely nothing he did eased the pain that she felt being with him... that is until she met Grief and had fallen head over heels in love with him.

No matter how much they tried to fight it, there wasn't any denying the chemistry between them. They wanted to be together, but Grief's loyalty to Khaza wouldn't allow him to cross that line. The OG was nothing more than a nickel and dime hustler from the streets of East Oakland until the drug lord gave him a shot at being in his empire. He seemingly went from rags to riches overnight and solidified his position in the organization. It was from this opportunity that Grief felt that he would be betraying the man that had blessed him. Although he and Rose had been in love and had been having sex quite frequently, he decided to sever their ties and go back to how things were. It wasn't until one night that he was asked to take Rose shopping and saw the injuries she sustained from his boss beating her that he knew that he had to do something or risk losing the woman that he loved.

Grief's eyes went back and forth between the rearview mirror to Rose, who was in the backseat. She wore oversized designer shades, and her hair was down to cover most of her face. He noticed that she had been avoiding eye contact since she'd boarded the Benz and had barely spoken a word to him. Grief's eyelids narrowed into slits, seeing bruising just below the lens of her right eye. Abruptly, he slammed on the brakes and startled her, jerking her forward. She looked around nervously, wondering what the hell was going on. Before she knew it, he was jumping out of the vehicle and heading to the backdoor where she was sitting. He opened the door and climbed inside, slamming the door shut behind him. He went to remove her shades, but she turned her face, ashamed to let him see what her piece of shit husband had done to her.

"It's okay, sweetheart."

Grief placed his hand on top of hers reassuringly. Taking a deep breath, she turned around to him. They were face to face. He slid the shades off her face and set them aside.

"Jesus," he said. Lines formed across his forehead when he saw what had been done to Rose's face. He turned her chin from left to right, getting a good look at the injuries she'd sustained by her husband's hands. Her eye was blackish blue and swollen shut. Her lip was busted, and the side of her face was swollen. She looked like she'd had an allergic reaction to something.

"What happened this time?"

"He got pissed 'cause I didn't want to have sex with him," she confessed, eyes twinkling with tears. Her bottom lip quivered, and she looked like she was about to cry. Fighting back her moment of weakness, she blinked back the wetness in her eyes and sniffled. Grief affectionately rubbed the side of her face and looked her in the eyes, a stern expression across his face.

"He tried to force me to go down on him, but I wouldn't."

There was silence as he stared past her, even though he was facing her. His eyes became glassy, his nostrils flared, and his top lip twitched angrily. The thought of Khaza putting his hands on the woman he loved fucked with his mind, body, and soul.

"Grrrrrr," Grief snapped and swung his fist into the tinted window, cracking it into a spider's cobweb. His violent tantrum startled Rose again. She watched as he pulled his fist back, glass particles trickling to the floor. He opened and closed his fist, looking at the tiny cuts in his knuckles. She tried to examine his hand, but he stopped her.

"I'm fine."

He shut his eyelids briefly and took a couple deep breaths, calming himself down. Afterwards, he pulled his cell from within the confines of his white suit. He dialed up his left and right hands, Fat Rat and Buddah. They worked under him for Khaza.

"Yo, we've got a situation..."

After the OG gave his niggas the rundown on what was about to go down, they were pulling up twenty minutes later, and all were driving back to their boss's mansion.

Rose was staring out of the passenger side window when Grief finally pulled up to her husband's mansion. She glanced out the back window and saw the BMW that Fat Rat and Buddah were in. She couldn't quite see what they were doing, but by their movements, she concluded that they were loading up their guns. The click clack of Grief chambering a live round into his own weapon brought her attention back around to him. She was just in time to see him resting the banger on his lap and turning around to her, seriousness bleeding from his vengeful eyes.

"I'll be right back, baby."

"What are you going to do?"

A worried expression crossed her face. He didn't utter a word as he stared into her eyes. It was through this direct eye contact that she understood that he was going to murder her husband. Suddenly, she hugged him tightly and tears spilled down her cheeks. When she pulled away, she held the sides of his face and kissed him romantically. They kissed twice more before he threw open the door and hopped out, expensive hard bottom shoes gracing the cobble stone driveway. She watched as he and his niggas joined up. They tucked their bangers in their waistlines and approached the front door. Grief knocked and looked around as he waited for someone to let them inside. Not a minute later, the butler was opening the door, and they were rushing inside, pulling their weapons back out.

Sitting up in the backseat with her eyes glued on the front door, Rose shut her eyelids and held her hands together. As tears ran down her face, she prayed to the Lord above to protect Grief and his niggas. Still reciting her prayer, she heard Grief and her husband exchanging heated words. Then, there were the raised voices of their men, and then came the excessive gunfire. The gunshots startled her, and more tears ran down her face, but she kept on praying. The firefight stopped, and the night became silent. As soon as Rose peeled her eyelids open, Khaza came staggering out of the front door holding a gun in his fist. A shocked expression was on his face, and a crimson stain was on his chest. His mouth quivered, and his grip loosened on his burner. It hung on by his finger. It fell and clasped down the steps. Right after, Grief came running out of the door, eyes burning with hatred. He lifted his banger at the nigga's back and pulled the trigger.

Blocka! Blocka! Blocka! Blocka!

He cut Khaza's ass down and sent him sliding halfway down the steps, droplets of blood splattering below his head. Grief stood where he was breathing hard with his gun still pointed down at him. His white suit was splotched with blood stains. The sound of more gunfire snapped him out of his thoughts. He ran back inside of the mansion and motioned for Fat Rat and Buddah to follow him. They came running out of the mansion, going their separate ways, heading to their respective cars. Fat Rat and Buddah jumped back inside of the vehicle that they came in, and Grief hopped back behind the wheel of the Benz, firing it up. He looked back and forth between the windshield and Rose, who was crying frantically.

"Thank God you're alive," she exclaimed as she threw her arms around him and kissed him all over his face. When those first wave of shots went off, she thought her man had gotten the business, but when she saw him run out of the mansion, she was relieved.

"Muah! Muah! Muah! Muah!"

Grief cracked a grin and passed his lady his crimson stained ratchet.

"Place that in the stash box, baby."

He pressed the buttons that activated the place where the drivers of the vehicle hid their weapons. As soon as it opened, Rose placed it inside, and he shut it. He then whipped out his handkerchief and passed it to her. She used it to wipe off her hands and stashed it inside of her bag.

"You're my lady now, okay?" Grief said, looking between the windshield and Rose. She nodded in agreement.

"Should anyone violate you, they gotta see me, and they gone get the same thing that cock sucka, Khaza, got. You hear me?"

"Yes, baby."

She continued to kiss his face.

"I love you, Bernard."

"I love you too, my darling Rose... my beautiful black darling Rose."

He took his eyes off of the streets for a second to kiss her lips. Using a curled finger, he took another look at the injuries she'd gotten from Khaza's crazy ass beating her. Looking at her face made him angry all over again. He couldn't understand how someone could hurt someone so sweet, kind and beautiful.

"Punk ass mothafucka... I should turn this bitch around and blast on his ass again."

He pounded his fist against the steering wheel as he clenched his jaws.

"No...don't."

She interlocked her fingers with his and lay back in the front seat, kissing his knuckles.

"It's all over now. I'm free, and we can be together... all of us."

She placed his hand on her stomach and rubbed it up and down, smiling. A big ass smile spread across Grief's face.

"You mean...you mean... my baby is having my baby?"

"Mmm hmm," she smiled and showed off her dimples, just as excited as he was. Grief pulled the car over to the side of the street and grabbed her by the face, kissing her hard and lovingly. He then held her by the stomach.

"Wait a minute… are you sure it's mine?" he asked as his brows furrowed.

"Positive," Rose spoke seriously and was telling the truth. She hadn't laid with Khaza since she started sleeping with Grief. Once the two of them had started their affair, she vowed to give her body to him and only him…her one true love.

"Is that why you refused to sleep with him?"

She nodded her head rapidly and said, "Yes… you and the life growing inside of me. Not only would that be disrespectful to you, but to our lil' prince or princess as well."

Grief stared into his lady's eyes as tears slid down his cheeks unevenly. He caressed her cheek with the side of his hand. He couldn't get over how a flower so delicate and beautiful could grow in a world so ugly. It was then that he vowed to protect her with his life.

"Thank you, baby."

"For what, my king?" she frowned, holding his hand to the side of her face, rubbing it against her cheek. When she spoke, he cried harder and bit down on his bottom lip. This caused fresh tears to flood her cheeks.

"Baby, tell me why are you thanking me? And why are you crying?"

"I'm crying for you, 'cause I wasn't there to protect you, and I'm thanking you for protecting our child from that bastard," he admitted. Immediately, she hugged and kissed him.

"You would have done the same. I have no doubt in my mind about that."

She took the scarf from around her neck and dabbed his face dry before wrapping it around his neck. She traced his face with her finger and then kissed his lips again.

"So what do you wanna name the baby?" she inquired, watching him pull off his bloody clothes and stash them in a bag which he also hid inside the stash box.

"If it's a boy, we'll name him after me, but if it's a girl... Treasure," he said, settling in the driver seat, having stashed his soiled clothing. Rose frowned as she laid her hands on top of his hands which were on her stomach. She gave him a look that questioned why he wanted to name their child Treasure should she be a girl.

"'Cause you guarded her like she was just that, baby...a treasure."

A smile spread across her lips, and her face lit up.

"I love it."

Grief kissed her on the cheek and fired up the Benz, pulling back into traffic. Driving, he smiled while listening to Rose sing a lullaby and rub her stomach. She watched the streets pass her by and occasionally glanced down at her stomach, thinking of the life blossoming inside of her.

That night, Grief and Rose took a jet out to Las Vegas where they got married. They enjoyed their honey moon and shot back to East Oakland where the OG established his dominance in the drug game. Niggas respected his empire or got dealt with. Mothafuckas had to take a knee and kiss the pinky ring. It was as simple as that.

Grief sat the portrait of his wife down on his desk top and took a sip of his hard liquor. He shut his eyelids briefly and clenched his jaws, feeling the hot liquid set fire to his throat on its way down to his stomach. Peeling his eyelids open, he licked his lips and sat his glass down. Rising to his feet, he approached the pyramid of photos that he had created. The photographs were of all of the men that he was associated with… ally or enemy. Most of the photos wore a red X over them. These were the men and women that he believed didn't have anything to do with his wife being murdered. The only photos that didn't wear a red X over them were Pain, Epic, Lil' Joe, Buddah, and Fat Rat.

The OG drew a red X over Pain's photo, capped his Sharpie marker, and tossed it upon his desk top. Staring at the photos, he massaged his chin. It was without a shadow of a doubt that one of the men in the photographs before him were responsible for the murder and rape of his wife.

CHAPTER FIVE

That night

Man, this fool was supposed to have been here, Lil' Joe thought to himself from the driver seat, head on a constant swivel as he took in all of his surroundings. He was sitting in the front passenger seat of Epic's money green box Chevrolet on chrome twenty-four inch rims. The cat that he was supposed to meet that night was forty minutes late, and he'd grown tired of waiting. He knew within his heart that if it wasn't for homie having such good coke on deck that they would have been stopped fucking with him. Fortunately, that wasn't the case.

Lil' Joe took a deep breath of frustration and picked his half smoked blunt from out of the ashtray. He stuck it in between his fat lips and brought the flame of his Bic lighter to it. It sizzled, and the end of it turned ember, smoke rising into the air. Tossing the lighter upon the passenger front seat, he went to take a pull from his bleezy and looked up into the rearview mirror. He released a cloud of smoke when he saw two white orbs heading in his direction. A slight smirk appeared upon his lips, seeing that it was the man that he was supposed to see. Hurriedly, he took one last pull from the end of his blunt and blew smoke from out of his nose and mouth. After mashing out what was left of what he was smoking, he adjusted his banger on his waistline and hopped out of his ride. A silver Buick LaSabre had just pulled up beside his Chevy when he was coming around the end of it. The driver side door of the Buick opened, and a handsome middle-aged Mexican man stepped out, one Mauri gator at a time. He was wearing a dark purple button down shirt that he had tucked in and matching slacks. A black leather belt held up his pants. Its buckle was a human skull. He wore a matching ring on his right hand.

"Manolo, what's up with it?"

Lil' Joe slapped hands with the plug and embraced him.

"Same ol' same ol'… anotha day, anotha dolla, poppa."

His thin lips stretched across his face to form a million dollar smile.

"Your jefe couldn't make it?"

He looked around for the young man's boss like he was expecting him to come strolling out any minute then, but nothing like that ever happened.

"He couldn't make it. He had some other business he had to handle," he let him know.

"But don't sweat it. One monkey doesn't stop no show. We gone still do business as long as you got the goods."

"I got the goods. Do you have the fedia?"

"Yep."

Lil' Joe popped the trunk and grabbed a duffle bag, unzipping it. He let Manolo see what was inside and he smiled, pleased at what he saw. Afterwards, he zipped the bag back up and held it at his side, slamming the trunk shut.

"Now, what chu got for me?"

Manolo popped the trunk and revealed two duffle bags. He unzipped each one and opened them up for Lil' Joe to see. Afterwards, he zipped the bags back up. Lil' Joe smiled like he was pleased with the contents the bags.

"There you have it, my friend. Thirty ki—"

Blowl!

The gunshot echoed through the area, startling Lil' Joe and dropping Manolo where he stood. He crumbled to the ground and twitched every so often. Lil' Joe stared down at his prone body with speckles of blood and brain fragments stuck to his face. His eyes were wide in shock, and his mouth was quivering just as his hands were. He couldn't believe what the fuck just happened before his very eyes. Still visibly shaken, he looked up from the twitching form of the man to a pair of evil eyes above a black bandana. The drawstrings of the gunman's hoodie were pulled so tight that it hugged his head like a latex condom. This was Epic. He paid Lil' Joe no mind as he stood over his victim and finished giving him something that would leave him lying still forever.

Blowl! Blowl! Blowl! Blowl!

The golden muzzle flashes illuminated his face. When he brought the gun down, the smoke trailed along with it, and he finally looked up at Lil' Joe's shocked expression. From the look on the Epic's face, it appeared like he was contemplating on clapping his little ass too. It wasn't until he tucked the warm gun on his waistline that the youngster sighed with relief.

"Tighten up, lil' nigga. You shakin' like Michael J. Fox," Epic capped, pulling the bandanna down around his neck and snatching up the duffle bags that Manolo had brought to make the exchange. Looking at the corpse caused Lil' Joe's jaws to swell, and he vomited, plastering the surface. Seeing this, Epic twisted up his lips and shook his head pitifully.

"I must say, lil' bro... I'm terribly, terribly disappointed with you. You out here losin' yo' lunch ova this dead spic. You act like you neva seen a dead body before."

"Ughhh," Lil' Joe brought his head back up and wiped his mouth with the back of his fist, looking up at that nigga like he'd lost his mothafucking mind.

"What the fuck you kill 'em for?"

"He was a means to an end."

He threw his arm around Lil' Joe's shoulders like a big brother would his little brother.

"Besides… a dead man tells no tales, yah mean?"

Lil' Joe didn't say shit. His head was hung low, and he was staring at his trembling hands. Seeing this caused Epic to scowl and press his ratchet underneath his chin, lifting his face up. Now that he had his undivided attention, he looked him square in the eyes and said, "Now, I'm gonna repeat what I just said again, and then you're gonna answer me, 'cause should you not, I'ma have yo' brains shooting out the top of your skull, ya understand me? Here we go."

He cleared his throat and started from the top with what he had first said.

"He was a means to an end. Besides… a dead man tells no tales, yah mean?"

"Right, right," Lil' Joe responded and shut his eyelids briefly, swallowing hard and nodding his head rapidly. Epic had ducked off to take a piss just before Manolo had shown up. Relieving himself, he tried to decide whether he was going to stick to his original plan of robbing the plug or letting that shit ride. Ultimately, he went along with his plans, figuring that he could come off with the money and the bricks, that way, he and his crew could be ahead in the game. They could use the money to buy off another plug while the drugs he stole kept the streets eating. Now, Epic knew that Pain wouldn't be down with his plan, but he was confident that he could get Lil' Joe's weak ass to go along with what he had in mind.

."That a boy,"

He patted his cheek like an old Italian mob boss and smiled, showcasing the gap between his top row of teeth. He then walked over to Manolo's ride and popped the trunk. He kept his eyes on Lil' Joe as he lifted the trunk open and dropped the duffle inside. The little nigga dropped his inside as well.

"Get in the car. I'ma handle this."

Lil' Joe climbed into the passenger seat and slammed the door shut. Looking through the side view mirror, he saw Epic pull a small thirty-two pistol from his ankle holster and place it into Manolo's hand, cracking a shot off. Afterwards, he took a wad out of his pocket and popped the rubber-band, spreading the bills about. Once he was done, he stood where he was to make sure it looked like a drug deal gone bad.

Visibly shaken, Lil' Joe looked to his trembling hands. He jumped when Epic jumped back inside of the car and slammed the door shut. He shut his eyelids for a second and sighed, relieved that he wasn't under attack. Epic looked at him like *you mothafucking pussy* before firing up the Chevy and driving off.

****

Epic decided to drive, since Lil' Joe had been acting kind of funny after he blew Manolo's brains out. Every so often, he found himself glancing over at him, taking his eyes off of the road ahead of him. The little nigga was trying to keep himself calm and was doing a piss poor job at it. His eyes had a glassy look to them, and he couldn't stop himself from quivering and looking at his shaky hands every five minutes. Trying to get a grip, he squeezed his eyelids shut and balled his hands into fists. He bit down on his bottom lip and willed himself still as best as he could, but there wasn't any use. He still slightly rocked.

One thousand and one thoughts went back and forth through his mind. For some reason, he kept seeing everything that lead up to Manolo's head exploding that day. Trying to decipher its meaning, he came up with the conclusion that he was experiencing everything that was eventually leading up to his last days on earth. This was because he knew that the Forty Thieves were a band of miscreants whose name was synonymous with ghastly murderers. He once heard about them skinning a man alive and leaving him hanging upside down from a tree in a busy intersection off of Crenshaw Blvd. The dude was one of their own, back when they were called the Forty-One Thieves. The poor bastard made the poor decision of stealing from out of the same bag that his comrades were eating out of.

Lil' Joe couldn't help thinking that if they had done that to one of their own people, that there wasn't any telling what they'd do to Epic and him if they found out they were involved in Manolo's murder. The thought alone had him sick to his mothafucking stomach.

"Pull ova!" he told Epic, cheeks swelling and shrinking. His eyes were bulging as he smacked his hand over his mouth.

"For what?" Epic asked, glancing back and forth between him and the windshield.

"I gotta throw up."

Epic pulled the box Chevy over alongside the curb that a tree resided on. The tree's leaves overshadowed the vehicle, casting a shade on it. Lil' Joe threw the passenger side door open and stuck his head out, unleashing a brownish orange goop. It splattered on the ground, and he kept on vomiting, splattering more and more. The veins on his neck and forehead swelled as he continued to spill his lunch. Epic made an ugly face and looked away, seeing all that his little home boy had barfed up. Lil' Joe spat up the last of the contents of his stomach and then wiped the slobber that hung from his bottom lip with his fist.

Lil' Joe ducked back inside of the car and pulled his legs in slowly like he was exhausted. Once he'd slammed the door shut behind him, he laid his head back against the headrest and his eyelids narrowed into slits. He sat there moaning and shit, feeling drained of his energy. Throwing up had taken its toll on him. With his head slightly turned, Epic gave Lil' Joe the evil eye and twisted his lips. He already knew what time is was with his little homie. His ass was scared of the repercussions that were going to come behind whacking out that fool, Manolo. It didn't even matter to him that he told him that he had all the bases covered when it came to that situation. He knew this because the youth was still spooked. Keeping his watchful eye on Lil' Joe, Epic pulled his nine-millimeter Beretta from its hiding place and sat it on his lap, finger curling around the deadly weapon's trigger.

He couldn't afford for Lil' Joe to bitch up and go running his mouth to Pain before he had all of the pieces on the chess board lined up to his liking. Nah… if that was to happen, then his entire house of cards would come crashing down. While Lil' Joe was sitting there moaning with that nasty looking shit he'd just thrown up at the corners of his mouth, Epic crept his ratchet up toward Lil' Joe's temple. As soon as he felt that cold gun metal at his temple, little homie's eyelids stretched wide open, and his mouth quivered. His eyes shot to their corners, and his heartbeat sped up.

"Wha...what the fuck you doing, man?" Lil' Joe asked, scared as shit.

"I know yo' punk ass, LJ. You ain't cut like that, homes. You gone fuck around and tell Pain every mothafuckin' thang, and I can't allow that to happen. I mean, look at chu, man. You all discombobulated and shit... throwin' up every fuckin' where."

Epic looked him up and down with disgust.

"Nah, nah, nah, big bro. It's just that I ain't never seen a nigga get his head blown off in front of me, is all. That shit fucked my head up. That's why I'm all shaken up and shit."

He shut his eyelids and continued to shake all over, swallowing his spit, his throat rolling up and down his neck.

"Look, just gimme a lil' something to get my mind right, and I'll be straight."

"Somethin' like what?"

He gave him the side eye and pressed his ratchet further into his temple, bending his head at an angle.

"What...whatever you got, man."

Lil' Joe's eyes were at their corners, and sweat was threatening to drip from off of his brow. Epic mad dogged Lil' Joe for a minute, mulling things over in his mind. He could go ahead and peel the little mothafucka's onion, but he didn't want his death on his conscience. The next best thing for him to do was to keep him high... so high that he wouldn't be able to function enough to tell anyone about the plan he had orchestrated. A slight smirk curled the corner of Epic's lips. He nodded his head and massaged his chin, eyes going to their corners. A scandalous thought entered his mental, and he snapped his fingers.

"Alright. Look inside of that glove box there. I got a lil' somethin', somethin' for you."

Lil' Joe went to reach for the glove box just a little too fast for Epic's taste, and he pressed his banger further into his temple.

"Ah, ah, ah, nice and easy, my nigga... nice and easy."

Lil' Joe shut his eyelids for a second and took a deep breath, moving slower this time. He opened the glove box, and inside he found three five dollar pieces of crack. The meat of his brows mushed together, and he looked to his big homie who nodded to him. This signaled to him to get the drugs out which he did.

"Get the stem out, too."

"Hold up. You mean for me to smoke this shit?" he looked at him like You can't be serious.

"LJ, you are one brilliant mothafucka. Now, how did you put two and two together like that?" he asked and gave him a sarcastic ass look.

"Man, you know this ain't my get down?" Lil' Joe complained with furrowed brows.

Whack!

Epic struck him upside his mothafucking head with the butt of his gun. His head flew forward, and a gash opened at the back of his skull. He squeezed his eyelids shut from the throbbing pain, touching the back of his head and coming away with blood. He looked at his red fingertips and couldn't believe that his big homie had cracked him upside his dome. When he looked at him, his eyes were threatening, and his lips were twisted. His nostrils contracted, and he clenched his jaws hard, displaying the structure of his bones.

"I ain't playin' no mo' games witcho mothafuckin' ass," Epic assured him. His hand was so tight on his gun that he was sure the weapon's handle had imprinted in his palm.

"Now, it's either this gun or the crack. Pick yo' poison, nigga!" he told him through gritted teeth.

Shit, that was a no brainer for Lil' Joe. He picked the narcotic. Effortlessly, he put the crack into the marred stem that he was handed from out of the ashtray. After fishing the Bic lighter from out of his pocket, he placed its flame to the front of the stem. Epic smiled wickedly and licked his slips, seeing him staring at the head of the stem. Lil' Joe saw the glass glow ember and saw the drugs inhabiting it sizzle and give birth to smoke. Right after, he was taking deep pulls, vacuuming the intoxicating smoke into his lungs.

"That's it. There you go. It isn't so bad is it?"

Epic lowered his gun and observed Lil' Joe. He was lying back in his seat. His eyelids were shut, and his lips were slightly parted, enjoying the sensation that the narcotic brought him. Lil' Joe had never gotten high before, but he saw his mom getting fucked up all the time. She was so strung out on crack that she was willing to do anything to get more of it, including pimping her ten-year-old son. Lil' Joe knew the horrors of child prostitution all too well. He endured it until Child Protective Services seized him from the home at twelve years old. They locked up his mother and placed him in a foster home.

"All right."

Epic stuck his banger back into its hiding place.

"We're going to holla at Pain. I'ma tell 'em what happened tonight. You just agree with everything I say. You got that?" Lil' Joe, eyelids still shut and lips still apart, nodded his head slightly.

"Good."

Epic cranked up the car, pulling away from the curb and into the street. Speeding, he traveled alongside the white line in the street, wind blowing inside and ruffling his shirt. He fished the half smoked blunt out from the ashtray. He glanced back and forth between the windshield and the bleezy between his lips, lighting it with the Bic lighter that his little homie had used. Smiling fiendishly, he looked up into the rearview mirror and saw interchangeable faces of himself and devil.

****

"Wait right here. I'll be right back," Epic ordered Lil' Joe before he hopped out of the Chevy. He looked both ways before jogging across the street, being as careful as he could. The neighborhood was scarcely lit due to every other light post bulb being blown out. This was because the niggas that were hustling on the corners had busted them out. They had done this so the police couldn't see them slinging crack out there. Coming upon the curb, Epic approached the gate of a Spanish stucco house. He entered the front yard and hustled up the stairs. When he reached a black iron door, he knocked on it and waited for someone to answer. While he waited, he occasionally glanced at the block behind him to make sure there wasn't anyone trying to make him a statistic. He was well aware of all of the murders that had occurred on that street. That was the reason why the residents had nicknamed it Murder Ave.

Epic turned back around just in time to hear the thick wooden door being unlocked and pulled open. A light shone at the back of the person that had pulled it ajar. He could tell by their silhouette that they were rocking a durag and by the repugnant cloud surrounding him that they were getting high.

"'Sup, blood?" durag greeted him, taking a pull from the withering joint pinched between his fingers. He knew Epic from around the way. He used to buy weed from him to smoke with the little hood rats he fucked with around the corner.

"It's Epic. Open up the mothafuckin' doe! Got a nigga standin' out here like he the Rollers and shit."

His eyebrows sloped and wrinkles went across the beginning of his nose.

"Who dat?" Epic heard someone call out. He couldn't see him from where he was, but he knew that he was on the couch alongside a host of others. He could tell by the sounds coming from the TV and all of the commotion that they were watching the basketball game.

"Ya mammy, nigga," Epic said as he was let inside of the house by Nut. This was the nigga in the durag. The durag was red and so was his Kansas City Chiefs jersey.

The man that Epic insulted emerged from out of the living room. He was a portly fellow, at about five foot two. He sported a red bandana on his head, Aunt Jemima style. The hairs on his chest were exposed thanks to his wife beater. The black Dickie shorts he wore hung off of his ass and showcased his boxers.

"Who the fuck you think you—" Shorty's eyelids stretched wide open, and he gasped seeing Epic inside of his house. He swallowed the lump of nervousness that had formed in his throat. See, that nigga Epic had fronted the little man an eight-ball four weeks ago. When it was time for him to shoot him back that paper, the short mothafucka disappeared. He didn't answer the homie's calls or texts, and when he would drop by, he would have his baby mama lie and say he wasn't there, but this time, Epic had caught his ass slipping. What Shorty wasn't counting on was someone answering the door besides him. He could kick himself in the ass for not letting Nut know not to let Epic into the crib. If he would have had a heads up that he was coming, he would have shot his little ass out of the backdoor and went straight to his side bitch's house, but it was far too late now. It was time to pay the piper.

"Aye, uh... what's up, Epic... man?"

Epic threw his head back in greeting.

"'Sup with it, big dog?"

"Ain't shit, loved one," Shorty responded. He then looked to Nut who had opened up the door.

"Well, just don't stand there. See if the man wants something to smoke or drink."

Durag snatched the joint from his big chapped lips and angled his head, looking at him like he belonged in a straitjacket. He couldn't help himself. He had to say something on the matter.

"Mannnnn, who the fuck is—"

Shorty whipped around and got into Nut's face.

"Aye, aye, shut cho ass up. When you needed some place to stay, I gave it to you, right?"

Nut hung his head in shame and nodded.

"That's right. You came here assed out, no money, no nothing, and I accepted you, nigga. You gotta earn yo' keep 'round this bitch, so see if the man wants something to smoke or drink."

He scolded his baby mama's younger brother like he was a little ass boy. Nut walked over to a smiling Epic and shamefully asked him if he wanted something to smoke or drink.

"Yeah, lil' homie. Get a nigga a glass of ice water... none of that faucet shit either."

"All right."

He nodded and headed off into the bathroom. Once he was gone, Epic started back up with Shorty.

"Yo, I'ma use yo' bathroom. I gotta take a piss."

Not waiting to hear what he had to say about it, he turned around and headed down the corridor, occasionally looking over his shoulder to see if home boy was watching him. When he saw that he wasn't, he moved to do what he'd really came there to do. As he journeyed down the corridor, the noise behind him in the living room grew softer and softer. After taking another cautious look around to make sure no one was watching him, he dipped off inside of the master bedroom for a minute and came back out. Next, he went into the bathroom, handled his business, washed his hands and left, shutting the door behind him. Epic returned to the living room, rubbing his hands together and looking at the niggas gathered there. None of them were paying attention to him. They were all focused on the game on a big ass flat-screen television set... even that fool, Shorty.

"That's what I'm talm'bout, baby."

He smiled proudly, applauding his team.

"Yo, Shorty," Epic called for him. Shorty looked in his direction, and he motioned him over. Once the little dude was standing before him, he started in on him.

"Peep this."

He flicked his nose with his thumb and threw his arm around his shoulders, walking him toward the door.

"I'ma swing by here on the fourth next month. That's when yo' baby mama gets her stamps and shit, right?"

Shorty nodded.

"What she get... like five hundred and somethin' in stamps and cash?"

Shorty nodded again.

"Alright... you hit me with all that next month and the month after, and we straight."

He unlocked and unchained the door. Pulling the door open, he turned around to Shorty and raised his fist.

"Cool?"

"Cool."

Shorty broke into a wide smile, dapping him up.

"Okay then. Take it easy, pimp."

Epic patted him on the shoulder and went to leave again, but the little man called him back. He turned around raising his eyebrows.

"Thanks, man... I mean... for giving me a pass and shit. I heard how you give it up in these streets, so when you showed up, I just knew it was all over me."

"See, I'm not so bad, am I?"

"Not at all."

"I'm outta here, my nigga. See you on the fourth."

Epic shut the door behind himself. He made his way down the steps, smiling like he knew something that no one else did.

CHAPTER SIX

"Did I thank you for plugging me in with yo' pops yet?" Pain asked as he munched on fries. A smiling Treasure looked to the ceiling like she was thinking, holding a fry with ketchup on it.

"You know? Come to think about it... you didn't."

"Well, thank you," he said, eating the fry she fed him smirking.

"I gotta get chu something nice for helping me close the deal."

"Most def'. Hold on a second, babe."

She picked up a napkin and folded it. Leaning forward, she dabbed the specks of ketchup on the sides of his mouth, a concentrated expression on her face. Looking up at her, he smiled. When she was done, she sat the napkin aside.

"Okay. I got it."

She was about to lean back in her chair when she locked eyes with him as he was taking a sip of his milkshake. He sat his cup down, and their eyes studied one another, rediscovering all of the things that had drawn them to one another in the first place. They stared at one another admiringly, captivated by each other's essence. To them, it seemed as if the establishment's atmosphere turned into a dark sky. They leaned over the table, slowly coming in closer and closer, until finally, their lips mashed against one another. As soon as their tongues slithered out and met, they performed a romantic kiss and angled their heads. At that moment, fireworks shot off into the sky and exploded. Several colorful embers sprouted and fell like droplets of rain, casting small illumination on the couple's faces.

Treasure pulled back, smiling and wiping the corner of her mouth. When she rested her hand on the table, a grinning Pain outstretched his hand. He placed his curled finger underneath her chin and caressed it. This caused her to blush and look down at the table.

"What?" he asked, enchanted by her angelic face.

"Can I tell you something and you not think I'm try'na run game or some shit?"

He wore a dead serious expression on his face.

"It's a free country."

"You are, by far, hands down, the most beautiful woman that I have ever seen in my life."

She shot him a look like "nigga, please" and took his hand from underneath her chin.

"Really, Trip?"

"Awww, now you wanna call out a nigga's government and shit?"

He gave her an amused look.

"Yes. Really, Trip? You've known me nearly all of my life, and you just now realizing that?"

"Nope," he replied and wiped his mouth, balling up his napkin.

"I always thought you were the most beautiful woman that I'd ever seen. I just never told you."

"Oh yeah? Why is that?"

She took a bite of her fries.

"What chu think, lil' lady?"

He took a bite of his McDouble. Stunned, Treasure dropped her fry back on the cheese burger wrapper and smacked the crumbs off of her hands. She couldn't believe Pain.

"You mean to tell me that you were scared? As many females you done bagged and tagged, and you're afraid of lil' old Treasure Latrice Jones?"

She pressed her manicured hand to her chest.

"Uhh huh," he nodded, taking another bite. Wiping his mouth with a napkin, he continued.

"True enough, ya boy done had his fair share, but most of them were hood rats. There's a big difference between a lady such as yourself and a hood rat. I couldn't holla at chu the way that I do them. You feel me? I had to try a different approach. Right when I was going to make my move at that block party, that's when that shit popped off with Chauncey's old faggot ass."

"I see."

She picked up her McChicken sandwich and took a bite. Seeing that she had mayonnaise at the corner of her mouth, Pain used a napkin to dab it away.

"Damn."

"What?" Treasure's forehead crinkled.

"There's a lil' more at the corner of your mouth."

Wearing a concentrated look, he leaned closer and abruptly kissed her. This caused them both to smile and chuckle.

"I'll give it to you... that was slick... real slick. Give me some."

She extended her fist to him. He dapped her up.

"Now, I want a real kiss... not none of that sneak shit."

"Alright."

Pain leaned halfway in and stopped. Surprise went across Treasure's face.

"What is it?" she watched him fish around inside of his pocket.

"What are you doing?"

Pain pulled a bottle of Binaca from out of his pocket, causing Treasure to burst out laughing and smack her hand over her mouth.

"Nigga, I know you didn't."

"Yes in the fuck I did," he cracked a smile and held up the Binaca.

"I got love for you, lil' mama, but yo' breath kicking like Jet Li. Now, open up."

"You cold. You know that, right?" she pointed at him, an amused expression on her face.

"Yeah, yeah, yeah."

Pain took her by the chin and she opened her mouth. He sprayed her mouth twice, mist wafting in the air.

"Now, it's your turn, bruh."

She playfully snatched the Binaca and sprayed his mouth. Afterwards, they kissed long and hard.

****

Treasure and Pain came out of McDonald's holding one another's hand, occasionally glancing at one another and smiling as they walked along.

"What?" he asked her, catching her smiling at him again.

"Nothing," she shook her head, smiling.

"Sooooo, where you wanna go to now?"

"I don't know. You decide. Ooooooh, I love this song."

She took him by his other hand and tried to get him to slow dance, hearing the music playing from a nearby night club. She placed one of his hands on her hip while she held the other one up with her left hand. Staring into his eyes, she told

him how to move and stole glances at his shoes. He was excited to see himself dancing, because that really wasn't what he did. The way he saw it, gangstas didn't dance. They did everything but that.
"There we go. Now look... you're a fast learner."
"Bet cho ass I am. I ain't no dumbass nigga. What chu thought?"
"Uhhhh, I thought just that," she chuckled in his face.
"Fuck you," he chuckled. She chuckled too.
"I'm just fucking witchu."
They slow danced, spinning around and around, staring into one another's eyes. Pedestrians crossing back and forth down the sidewalk moved out of the way and looked at them like they were crazy, especially with them both humming the tune playing from the night club. Suddenly, they stopped, panting and out of breath a little bit, staring into one another's eyes again. Pain slipped a curled finger underneath Treasure's chin and pulled her closer. They shut their eyes as they kissed again. The experience was just as amazing as the last time that they'd kissed inside of McDonald's.
Seeing something out the corner of his eye, Pain turned around and saw the most beautiful guitar inside of a pawn shop's window. It was brown, burnt orange, and yellow. The lights that were focused on it really played up the instrument's appearance. It looked like it belonged in the hands of a superstar guitarist. A "For Sale" sign was on the guitar for $200. Treasure looked back and forth between Pain and the marvelous instrument. He seemed to be under the guitar's hypnosis, drawing him to it like a moth to a flame. The thug shuffled toward the window, moving like a zombie.
"Hmmm."

Treasure's forehead wrinkled, and she angled her head, seeing all of this occur. She couldn't help wondering the connection between the thug and the fancy instrument. She'd seen niggas in love with money, cars, jewelry and women, but never a guitar before.

Pain pressed his face and palms against the window. His breathing fogged up the glass. His eyes were stretched wide open. The sexy instrument had him held hostage and wasn't trying to let him go. It looked exactly like the one an old friend had given him years ago. Pain had been in love with guitars since he was a little kid. He used to walk around with a miniature one he'd gotten for Christmas in the group home when he was a little boy. He barely knew how to play the thing, but he practiced as much as time permitted it. It wasn't until him and Skylar were out on the streets that they ran into this old man that was playing a guitar out in front of the club for profit, that he learned how to play the instrument with expertise. Sometimes, the old man would let him do a full hour show, and whatever proceeds he earned, he'd let him keep it all to himself. Pain always broke bread with him though. The way he saw it, you looked out for those that looked out for you. A few months later, the old stud let him have the guitar as a birthday gift.

One night, the old man had decided to let Pain play to hustle up enough money for him and Skylar a hot meal. While the young nigga played, the old man would play the harmonica and tap his foot, creating their own music. Pain busted a cold ass freestyle about struggling to survive in the streets, and the old dude came behind him with the hook.

Anyway, while they were performing, a couple of crackheads ran up on them with knives. They stabbed the old head up and took the guitar case of earnings they'd made. When they tried to take the guitar, the young nigga put up a fight and ended up getting stabbed in the hand three times. He was rushed to the emergency room in an ambulance, but the old dude didn't make it. Pain would never forget his name though. He called himself Fats. The youngster had even gotten a mural tattooed on his arm in his memory. The piece was astonishing and Pain's favorite.

For years, Pain wasn't able to play a guitar due to his wound. His hand would cramp up after a while, and he'd stop. He reasoned that the incident in front of the club was a sign from God for him to leave music alone and focus on what really paid, and that was hustling. Still, those nights when he and Epic were out in the streets trying to turn nothing into something, he'd find himself mentally recording songs he'd play with a guitar. However, with running the streets and chasing skirts, he didn't find the time to get back to playing. Hell, he'd forgotten about ever playing again... that was until he met Treasure, and she made him fall in love with music all over again.

Pain was so captivated by the instrument that he didn't come back to the realization of where he was until the owner was removing it and the "For Sale" sign along with it. He blinked his eyelids and looked around, frowning when he didn't see Treasure in sight. All he saw was vehicles coming up and down the street and pedestrians walking the sidewalk. He made his way to the entrance of the pawn shop. As soon as he reached the doorway, a smiling Treasure was coming out, holding the guitar like she knew how to play it. Pain was stunned when he saw her, all choked up and shit when she handed it over to him. He looked back and forth between her and the guitar, still stunned.

"Treasure, I...I don't know what to say."

He slowly began to toy with the strings on the instrument.

"Well..." she started off, still smiling as she stuck her hands in her jacket.

"... for starters, you can say thank you."

"Thank you."

He held the guitar with one hand and embraced her with the other, kissing her on the cheek.

"Thank you, thank you, thank you."

He went back to toying with the guitar's strings, a smile stretching across his lips.

"This is...this is the nicest thing that someone has ever done for me."

"Really?" her brows furrowed. She was surprised by this.

"Yeah," he nodded and flipped the guitar over. Once he flipped the guitar over and saw the faint traces of his name carved in it, he got weak in the knees. This was the same guitar that Fats had given to him for his birthday. At that moment, he came to the conclusion that the crackheads that had robbed him and the old man that night had pawned the instrument. It amazed him how the pawn shop hadn't sold it in all of these years. The only way he could make sense of it was that Fats was making shit happen from the heavens. When that thought came to mind, he looked up into the dark sky and thanked the man that had taught him how to play before looping the instrument's strap over his shoulders.

With emotional glassy eyes, Pain looked up at Treasure and told her the story behind the guitar. The tale brought tears to her eyes, and she asked to take another look at it, looping it over her shoulders and getting a feel for playing it. When she handed it back over to Pain, he kissed her and thanked her again. Wiping his eyes with the back of his fist, he went on to freestyle a song, walking alongside Treasure. It wasn't long before she broke out into a full song and dance. They performed a duet together, creating a song that anyone would love. They named it "A Love Like This".

I never thought I'd find a love like this
A love so true
I never thought my best friend's brother would become my boo...

These were the lyrics to the parts of the chorus that Treasure sung. Pain's lyrics to the chorus were slightly different.

I never thought I'd find a love like this
A love so true
I never thought my sister's best friend would become my boo...

Together they sung the last four bars. La-la-la-la-la-la-la-la...

Finishing their song, Pain and Treasure kissed and gave each other props.

"Aye, we don't sound bad together," Pain admitted.

"Gimme some."

He dapped her up and then looked around, lines creasing his forehead.

"Mannn, fucking with cho ass, I done walked ten blocks from my mothafucking car and shit," he laughed.

"Nigga, you started it with that punk ass guitar," she said and playfully punched him in the shoulder and laughed.

"Come on so that we can walk back."

She grabbed him by his hand and headed back in the direction that they came from. She took about five steps before he stopped her.

"Hold up. Fuck that. We're taking an Uber back."

He pulled out his cellular to make the arrangements for the ride through the application. Once he was done, he slid the device back into his pocket and told her that their ride would be there in four minutes. Abruptly, he winced and shook the hand he'd gotten stabbed in when he was a little nigga, trying to survive in the streets.

"You okay?" a frowning Treasure approached and took his scarred hand, caressing it. She looked down and saw the puncture wounds from when he'd been stabbed.

"This is the hand, huh?"

He looked up at her and nodded. He then looked back down at his hand as she began to massage it. It began to feel slightly better with her doing this to it.

"I got some lotion in my bag, I'ma massage your hand real good for you once we get into the Uber car."

"Thanks."

He kissed her cheek sweetly. She blushed.

"Don't mention it, love."

Right then, a Mazda 626 pulled up before them. Pain asked the dude behind the wheel if he was the nigga that the app said was going to pick him and Treasure up. He told him yes, and they hopped into the backseat. Treasure massaged her boo's hand on the drive back to his whip. He thanked her when they hopped out and told her that his hand felt better.

Afterwards, he was on his way to drop her off at her house. On the way there, Treasure noticed that Pain was texting someone and hardly paying attention to their conversation. She figured that he was entertaining the next bitch, and she was pissed off. Although she wanted to curse his ass out, she kept her emotions in check, because he wasn't officially her man.

When Pain pulled up in front of Treasure's house, he leaned over to kiss her goodnight, and she slammed the passenger side door in his face. His forehead deepened with creases, wondering what the fuck her problem was. Once he saw that she'd gotten inside of the house safe and sound, he drove off, replaying the night's events inside of his head. He couldn't think of any violation that he'd made.

Although Treasure was heated, her mood changed as soon as she opened her front door and saw all of the flowers she'd been delivered. There were roses all throughout the house, so much so that she had trouble walking around them. All she could do was smile and say wow, seeing all of those incredibly gorgeous arrangements. She snatched up a rose as she dialed up Pain, plopping down on the couch. Shutting her eyelids, she inhaled the wonderful scent and listened to his phone ringing. Finally, he picked up.

"*Yo' old sneaky ass... so that's what you were doing while you were on yo' cell?" she cracked a big smile.*

He laughed and said, "Yeah... I saw you getting all into yo' feelings and shit. I couldn't let chu in on what I was doing, 'cause it would have ruined the surprise, ya know?"

"Yeah, I feel you. Thanks for the roses. They're beautiful."

"Just like the woman that I sent them to."

She blushed and smiled harder.

"Stop it. You got me smiling and shit."

Tranay Adams

Pain and Treasure went on to talk for hours that night. They agreed to go out on another date since they'd enjoyed so much of each other's time.

The studio was dark, save for the big white wax candles that were scattered throughout, burning and illuminating light. Showtime stood behind Dead Beat who was working the control board for the music. The board was black and lit up with neon blue, green, and white lights. These two men were focused on the window of the booth where Treasure was standing before a microphone and holding the headphones to her ears. Her hair was done in crinkles, and she was wearing a T-shirt and white jeans that had tears going down their legs, leading down into black leather motorcycle boots. Her eyes were behind the tints of black shades which were there to hide the grief that she was experiencing while performing the song. They may have helped hide the pain in her eyes, but they didn't do anything from stopping the tears from sliding down her cheeks. Teardrops fell from her eyelids and pelted the yellow legal pad that sat on a stand just below her. Their wetness formed bubbles on the pages and caused the ink to run. Treasure had long ago stopped singing from the lyrics that she'd written to the beat and had taken to crooning straight from her heart. She was singing with so much passion and intensity that veins bulged at her temples and neck. She lifted her hand and balled it into a fist, hitting a high note that she pulled from within the depths of her stomach.

I say ooooooooh, you make me never wanna love agaiiiiiiiiiin

You hurt me at the core of my heart to the depths of my soullll

But I'd be lying if I said I don't love you no mo'

I say oooooooh, you make me never wanna love agaiiiiiiiiin
You hurt me at the core of my heart to the depth of my soullll
But I'd be lying if I said I don't love you no mo'
"That's right, baby girl. Let cho listeners feel that hurt... that pain...that anger in the song. Make them identify with what you have been through."

Showtime clenched his fist tightly, displaying the veins in his hands. With each word that he spoke, there was a glint of gold from the golden fangs inside of his grill. Showtime was a six-foot cat with a head as shiny as a bowling ball and a muscular body that filled out a charcoal gray suit. He wore a black turtle neck underneath his jacket and slip in leather shoes with hard bottoms. In one hand, he held a short staff that had a gold serpent's head on the top of it with rubies for eyes. The jewels twinkled under the candle light. This bald headed nigga was the C.E.O of Big Willie records, arguably one of the most successful recording companies since Death Row records. Upon meeting the multimillionaire, you would swear before your Lord and savior that he was a good dude, but truthfully, the scandalous mothafucka was a wolf in sheep's clothing. All he cared about was money and some more money, and anyone or anything that got in the way of that would be handled expeditiously.

"We got anotha one."

Dead Beat smacked his hands together and rubbed them excitedly. The corner of his lips curled in amusement. Dead Beat was a stocky white dude. He sported a fedora, a white V-neck, and baggy blue jeans. A wallet chain hung loosely from the front loop of his jeans and attached to his worn brown leather wallet that was stashed in his back pocket.

"You mothafucking right we do."

Showtime grabbed him by the face and kissed his cheek, tilting his hat to the side accidentally.

"Goddamn, Show."

Dead Beat frowned up and wiped his cheek with the back of his fist.

"You know yo' white ass is a genius for these beats you produce. You know that, right?" Showtime told him.

"Yeah, yeah, yeah."

He fixed his hat on his head and went back to listening to Treasure, toying with the controls on the board. A smirk was on his lips as he slightly shook his head, thinking that his boss was something else. Nonetheless, he loved the praise he got for crafting hit songs. Showtime glanced over his shoulder at his uncle.

"What chu think, Keith?"

"Every bitch that has experienced a heartache gon' feel this, no doubt," the tall, bald, earth toned nigga replied. He had platinum loop earrings in his lobes and a humongous icy platinum pinky ring. He was in a white T-shirt, black leather vest, and straight leg jeans. Snake skin cowboy boots graced his feet. Keith, or Crazy Keith as most called him, was Treasure and Showtime's bodyguard. He was an ex-street nigga that made his bones as a hired gun. All he knew was the streets and made his peace with dying in them until his nephew, Showtime, pulled him out of the gutter and gave him a legal way to make money.

"Alright, Treasure, bring it on home!"

Dead Beat rolled himself closer to the control board and adjusted a few things. Leaning back in the chair and clasping his hands behind his head, he shut his eyelids. He began nodding his head and tapping his booted foot on the carpet, merging himself in the music. Before long, Showtime and Keith were doing the same thing that he was doing. There was just something about the R&B diva's music that pulled you in. Even if you hadn't been through what she had, you could still feel whatever emotion the song presented when you were listening to it.

Once Treasure finished recording the song, she hung up her headphones and removed her shades. She then wiped the wetness from off of her cheeks and balled up the Kleenex. Sniffling, she slid the shades back on and strolled out of the booth. As soon as the door clicked shut behind her, she received applause and whistles from the men present.

"That was beautiful. Truly, truly beautiful, baby girl."

Showtime smiled, showcasing those infamous fangs of his.

"Thanks," she replied, screwing the cap off of a bottle of water and drinking. Once she'd had enough, she screwed the cap back on and started gathering her belongings. This caused Showtime's face to ball up. He wasn't pleased about her departure. He slid into her path to the door, hands up and palms showing.

"Hold up. Where are you going, lil' mama?"

"Shit, I'm leaving. I got a date tonight."

She slipped her other arm into the sleeve of her brown leather motorcycle jacket.

"What? You just got here an hour ago," he reminded her.

"No," she wagged her finger in his face.

"You mean *you* just got here an hour ago. Dead Beat and I have been here for hours putting in work."

She glanced up at the clock on the wall.

"I'm hungry, and I'm thirsty. I wanna take my pretty ass to a nice restaurant and get my mothafucking grub on. Now, if you'll excuse me."

She went to go around him, and he stepped in her path again. Her brows formed a slope, and wrinkles went across the beginning of her nose. She looked him up and down like *nigga, if you don't get the fuck up out of my face.*

"I'm sorry, baby girl…"

He laid his jeweled hands on her shoulders, slowly creeping them toward her neck. It seemed as if he was about to choke her, especially with that madness glinting in his eyes.

"… but I just can't allow you to leave like that. I'll tell you what, beautiful…lay down those other three songs that you and I discussed, and then, I'll let chu go on 'bout ya business."

At this point, his thumbs were on her throat, and his fingers were around her neck. He was so close to her that she could smell the expensive cologne expelling from him. His lips were peeled back in a devilish smile like he had something sneaky orchestrated. Even with the threat of being choked the fuck out looming in the air, Treasure didn't show any fear. Nah, lil' mama was a gangsta's daughter, so she was 'bout it like her old man. The princess of R&B's face morphed into a hateful guise, and she twisted her lips. Suddenly, Showtime's eyes bulged, and he gasped. Looking down, he saw that his artist had a Taser pressed against the bulge in his slacks.

"Get cho mothafucking hands from around my neck, nigga!"

She shot daggers at him, and he shot his hands in the air like the cops drew down on him and told him freeze.

"Now... I'm taking my ass home, and I'm not coming back to record 'til I feel like it... yah mean?"

"Baby girl, you tripping right now. Look... I can tell you're pretty tired, so why don't chu go on home, and hit the sack? We'll link up and finish this session some other time."

"Yeah, yeah... flip it all you want. I called this shot," she told him. Afterwards, she removed the Taser from his crotch and dropped it inside of her bag. Showtime shut his eyelids briefly and swallowed the spit in his throat, thankful that she didn't electrocute his ass.

Treasure's cellular rang, and she answered it, keeping her eyes on Showtime. He was feeling his crotch to make sure that his dick was okay.

"I'm finna step out now. Nah, you ain't stopping nothing. I'm outta here."

Treasure disconnected the call and stashed it in her bag. Having bid Dead Beat and Keith a farewell, she looked the owner of her label up and down, disgusted. She rolled her eyes and sucked her teeth before making her departure.

"Lil' mama told you, nephew," Keith said after seeing the exchange.

"Fuck off, old man."

Showtime adjusted his belt. His cellular rang, and he answered it, adjusting his slacks now.

"Speak to me," he spoke into the cell phone and listened to what he was being told. His face twisted tighter and tighter with anger, hearing the news that he'd been delivered.

"They had a meeting with Blessyn… Blessyn that's signed to my label?" he spoke like he couldn't believe it, squaring his jaws afterwards.

"Disloyal, fool ass nigga!"

Showtime launched his cellular at the wall, and it broke, crashing to the floor.

CHAPTER SEVEN

The elevator doors slid apart, and Treasure stepped out on level C of the parking lot complex. Coming out of the elevator lobby, she found a purple Lamborghini Gallardo idling before her. Its windows were limousine tinted, and its Carolina blue headlights appeared to glow in the dark. It was partially hidden within the shadows of the complex, its purple paint job standing out. She could hear the loud music that it housed trying to escape into the atmosphere.

Treasure got about halfway to the sports car before the driver side door opened, and the man behind the wheel stepped out. As soon as the door swung open, The Game's "One Blood" impregnated the area. A tall brown skinned nigga that resembled Tupac Shakur stepped out, one red Hush Puppy at a time. He made his debut, showing off what he'd chosen to wear that night. He sported a black brim with a red feather, a black silk shirt and slacks. Around his neck dangled two small gold Jesus pieces, one bigger than the other. On his wrist was a chunky Cuban link bracelet, and on his pinky was a ring with a capital B flooded with diamonds. Adjusting his brim, and then twisting his ring around his finger, he made his way around to the passenger side door. After he opened the door, he stepped aside and allowed Treasure access to the vehicle.

"'Sup, love?" Blessyn greeted Treasure. He leaned in for a kiss on the lips, and she turned her head, causing it to land on her cheek. Instantly, he frowned, wondering what he'd done to get her to be acting all funny with him and shit.

"You good, T?"

"Mmmm hmmm."

She ducked off inside of his whip, and he shrugged, shutting the door behind her. Afterwards, he ran around to the opposite side and jumped in, shutting his door. Blessyn pulled out into the street, making a turn at the end of the block. He sped through the streets as Treasure stared out of the passenger side window. She was watching the streets out of the limo tinted window, her reflection shown on the glass. The songstress wore a sorrowful look, eyes tearing. Teardrops rimmed her eyes, but she blinked them back. At the moment, she hated herself for missing Pain, but she couldn't help it. She was still very much in love with him. No matter how hard she tried, she couldn't get him out of her head. It was like he stayed with her like birth marks. Hell, the one reason she entertained Blessyn was so he'd keep him off of her mind. It worked for the first couple of days they were together, but then the love of her life kept coming to mind. She wanted so badly to go running back to him, but she knew that if she did that she'd look weak, and she couldn't have him looking at her as anything else but strong.

Treasure took a deep breath and expelled air. This caused Blessyn to look back and forth between her and the windshield, the meat of his forehead bunched together. Although he was wondering what was on her mind, he wasn't about to pry.

"Yo, I was thinkin' we hit up this lil' Mexican restaurant my reli told me about tonight. You down with it or what's up?"

"Sure," she replied nonchalantly, not bothering to look in his direction.

"Must be that time of the month or somethin'," he said under his breath, shaking his head disappointedly. He then cranked up the volume on the song that he was listening to when he scooped her up. Flooring the gas pedal, the Lambo took off through the city streets, making the lines dividing lanes appear as blurs.

****

Pain waltzed inside of the men's rest room at Raphael's, a five star Italian restaurant in North Hollywood off of Sunset Blvd. He moved past a white cat in an expensive tuxedo, brushing shoulders with him. The man excused himself, and the thug gave him a pardon, proceeding toward the first urinal alongside a row of others. He unzipped his jeans and pulled out his meat, throwing his head back and shutting his eyelids. The nigga took a deep breath and relieved his bladder, looking down to shake his dick once he was done. Once he put his shit back up, he flushed the urinal and headed to the sinks, clearing his throat with a fist to his mouth along the way. Stopping before one of the sinks, he turned the dial of the faucet and water flowed easily. Pumping the button on the dispenser, he held his palm under it and pink foam oozed out into his hand. He rubbed his hands together until they were masked white at their wrists. After that, he stuck his hands under the water and began rinsing them of the soap. While he was doing this, he occasionally looked up at the wall to wall mirror. All he could see, besides the doors of the stall behind him, was his own reflection.

It was at this time that he took the time to take in his appearance. Pain was a dark caramel skinned cat, with a fade that swirled with waves and a thick nappy beard, like those Philly niggas that pledged allegiance to Allah. The Holy Cross was tattooed at the corner of his right eye. He weighed all of two-hundred fifty pounds. His appearance was intimidating, but if you were blessed to receive a smile from him instead of a bullet, then you'd come to realize he wasn't that bad of a guy.

Having finished rinsing his hands, Pain turned off the faucet and walked over to the air dryer. Pressing the big metal button, the white machine came to life, blowing hot air downward. He was just about to stick his hands underneath it when a loud boom resonated throughout the restroom. His combat instinct kicked in, and he whipped around, reaching for the forty-five automatic on his waistline. He was about to pull out and make thunder roll until a man came inside the rest room with his drunken wife. Her eyes were big, and her jaws were as big as balloons, her hand pressed to her lips. The woman was running as fast as she could to one of the stall's doors. She shoved it open and dropped to her knees, spraying the bowl with vomit.

"I'm coming, honey. I'm coming!" her husband called out, running toward the stall that his wife had ran into. He stood over her and pulled her hair back into a ponytail so that her hair wouldn't get caught in the nasty goo that she spewed from within the depth of her disturbed stomach.

Seeing this, Pain took a deep breath and sighed with relief. The door banging up against the rest room's wall sounded like a gunshot from a large caliber weapon. On the spot, he was transported back to the night that he was shot and nearly died. At that moment, he crossed himself in the sign of the crucifix and looked up at the ceiling, thanking God for allowing him to keep his life. Having wrapped up his business in the rest room, Pain made his way toward the door and pushed it open. He crossed the threshold back inside of the restaurant where he saw his sister, Skylar, sitting at their table. The waiter had just arrived with their food and was sitting them down on the table top before their respective seats. Lastly, he placed a golden bottle of some very expensive champagne down.

"Is there anything else that you'd like, madam?" the waiter asked. He was a tall dude in a tie and button-down. A thin mustache resided over his top lip.

"No, that will be all. Thank you."

Skylar readied her napkin cloth.

"All right then. If you need anything, don't hesitate to summon me. Enjoy your meals."

He gave her a slight nod and went about his business. Pain approached the table, admiring his and his sister's plates, smiling. He picked up his cloth napkin and sat down.

"Looks good... looks really good."

Pain and his sister picked up their forks and indulged in their food. He had ordered the baked Ziti alongside garlic bread and a salad while she had spaghetti and meatballs. It had been quite some time since the siblings kicked it together, so tonight, they decided to go out to eat and catch up on one another's lives.

The siblings took a few bites of their meals before Skylar decided to pour up two flutes of champagne. Once the flutes were full of the golden alcohol, she sat the bottle aside. At the same time, she and her brother picked their glasses up and stared one another in the eyes.

"I'd like to propose a toast to family," she stated proudly.

"To family," he stated behind her.

"I love you, sis."

He tapped his fist against his chest.

"I love you too, bro bro."

She tapped her fist to her chest. They touched glasses and took a sip from their flutes, smiling. When Pain went to sit his flute down, the smile vanished from off of his lips. Across the room, he saw Blessyn and Treasure sitting at a table. Their waitress had just left their table which she'd placed their plates of food on. The crooner appeared to picking around the chicken salad she'd ordered from what he could tell, but Blessyn, on the other hand, was going to work on a juicy medium rare T-bone steak.

"What chu looking at, Trip?" Skylar asked with a jaw full of food. She'd just noticed the angered look on her brother's face. He nodded over her shoulder, and when she looked, she saw the cause of his sudden mood swing. The first thing she thought was *oh shit*. Words didn't have to be exchanged between her and her brother. Skylar already knew the history between her brother, Treasure, and Blessyn. When Treasure had caught him fucking around with her cousin, she was heartbroken and wanted revenge, so she fucked Blessyn to get back at him. Pain hated him because he was a rich arrogant thug that paraded around town like his shit didn't stink. The mothafucka looked down on everyone that wasn't holding a bag as large as his or larger than his.

When word got back to Pain about Treasure creeping with old boy, he was devastated, but he fronted to the princess of R&B like it was nothing. In the end, Treasure felt cheap, having given her body to another man just to get back at the man she loved. She vowed to stop fucking with Blessyn, but he was persistent. She eventually gave in and entertained him, figuring she'd use him as a rebound to get over Pain. Little mama didn't play with his heart though. She made sure that homie knew that their little thing was with no strings attached, so if he fucked around and caught feelings then that was all on him. Her conscience would be clean.

Skylar said fuck under her breath while her head was turned away from her brother. Fixing her face, she turned to Pain and squeezed his hand, trying to calm him down.

"Trip, let that shit go. You and I are here to have ourselves a good time. It's family day, remember?"

She patted his hand and looked him in the eyes. He was facing her, but his eyes were focused on Treasure and Blessyn. He licked his lips and cracked a toothy smile.

"Come on now, bro. Let that nigga breathe tonight."

For the first time, Pain looked at his sister, patting the hand that she had on top of his hand reassuringly.

"You worry too much, sis. A nigga ain't wetting that fool, Blessyn. As a matter of fact, to show you that I'm fine with how things turned out, I'ma send them a bottle of the most expensive champagne in this place and pay for their meals."

"Nigga, what?" Skylar tilted her head to the side and folded her arms across her chest, looking at him like he'd slipped and busted his head.

"Whatever you smoking on, let me know, so I know to stay my lil' ass away from it."

"Now you know I don't smoke," he told her, then scanned the restaurant for the nigga that was waiting their table. When he spotted him he called for him and snapped his fingers, motioning him to come over. Once the waiter arrived, Pain motioned for him to lean closer and he told him what he wanted done.

****

Blessyn was pleased with the dishes that the waitress had sat down before him and Treasure. He ordered a bottle of their finest wine and grabbed his napkin cloth. He and Treasure didn't waste any time digging into their meals.

"It's good, boo?" Blessyn asked as he munched hardily, looking up from his plate.

"Uhh huh."

Treasure glanced up at him and cracked a halfhearted smile, then went back to eating her food. She had a million things on her mind at that moment.

"Wine?" he held up the expensive bottle of wine.

"Sure."

She swallowed her food and held up her glass. He filled them both up. Blessyn's cellular rang and vibrated. Sitting the bottle of wine down, he pulled out his cell and looked at the screen. It said Showtime.

"Suck my dick, ol' bitch ass nigga," he spoke in a hushed tone, seeing the C.E.O of his label on the display. Afterwards, he stashed the device inside of his slacks and picked his glass up.

"Who was that?"

"Showtime."

He gathered food on his fork.

"You're not going to answer it?" she frowned.

"Nah, fuck that nigga, you know I'm leaving the label, right?"

"When?"

"Pretty soon. I'm just entertainin' offers from different labels," he spoke honestly.

"I'm seriously thinkin' about fuckin' with A1 though. I'm not for sure… ain't shit concrete."

"When Showtime finds out, he'll probably have you killed."

She was dead ass serious too.

"Fuck that slick talkin' pimp. That cock sucka ain't puttin' fear in nobody's heart ova here."

"I feel you."

"I'd like to propose a toast," he changed the subject, lifting his glass. She was right behind him, lifting hers too. They were about to touch glasses when the waitress came back over with a golden bottle of champagne. She sat it on the table top and told the gangsta rapper that the bottle and their meals were paid for.

"Paid for?"

Blessyn's forehead wrinkled, looking from the waitress to Treasure, and she shrugged.

"By who?"

"That gentleman over there."

The waitress smiled and pointed at Pain. The thug smiled and held up his flute. Pissed off, Blessyn motioned Pain over to his table. Pain rose to his feet, and Skylar grabbed him by the sleeve of his jacket, trying to stop him from going over there. He patted her hand and told her something that put her slightly at ease. With that, the nigga was en route in the gangsta rapper's direction, a serious expression written on his face.

"Blessyn, what' are you about to do?" a worried Treasure asked, grasping his hand.

"I just wanna holler at the nigga is all."

"Blessyn, seriously… don't start no—"

"My nigga," Blessyn began once Pain had stepped before him.

"Don't chu see me and my lady are try'na eat?"

Veins formed on his forehead, and his nostrils pulsated. His fingers pulled a steak knife into his palm and gripped it tightly.

"Yeah, I saw y'all over here try'na eat. I paid for your food, and I sent a bottle ova here. I would think a nigga could at least get a thank you... some type of appreciation or something. Damn."

He adjusted his jacket and thumbed his nose.

"Check this out, home boy. I'ma million dolla nigga. I don't need you or anybody else to pay a mothafuckin' thang for me."

Blessyn shot to his Hush Puppies, and Treasure grabbed his wrist. He snatched away.

"Now, I suggest yo' punk ass breeze, 'fore I carve yo' fuckin' heart out and eat that mothafucka!"

"Anytime you feeling froggy, bitch!" Pain snarled, top lip twitching angrily. Skylar came beside him, trying to stop him from doing something that he may regret. At the corner of his eye, he saw her saying something to him, but she may as well have been invisible as far as he was concerned. The only thing he heard, or saw, was the nigga that was standing before him... Blessyn.

"Fuck this shit!"

Blessyn kicked over the table. It crashed to the floor, and so did plates and glasses, shattering into pieces. Treasure stood up and backed away, shocked at what had just occurred. The music was cut inside of the establishment, and the patrons were focused on the drama that was unfolding.

"You're a dead man, home boy!"

His hand shot out, and he pointed the steak knife at Pain. Veins throbbed at his temples and neck. His nostrils were flaring, and his jaws were clenched.

"I'ma kill you, cock sucka!"

"Stupid ass nigga… you brought a knife to a gunfight?"

Pain held his leather jacket aside and exposed his forty-five automatic handgun. The moment Blessyn wanted to try his luck at a game of chance, he was going to clap that ass up.

"By the time you go to strike, I would have been put three holes in yo' fucking head."

"We'll see, blood! Grrrr," Blessyn went to stab the shit out of Pain. This made Treasure look at his ass like he needed to be committed to an insane asylum.

"Yep."

Pain lifted that thang off of his waistline and was about to set it off when a voice came from his right. He kept his burner on his enemy, and his enemy kept his knife on him. Both their eyes said that they were both willing to kill and die right there inside of that restaurant. The street niggas stayed stuck in these poses as the voice that had rang out continued to speak.

"Gentlemen, I have called the police. It is in both of your interest to leave here now," the short, medium built manager informed them. He was in a cheap black suit and shoes, sweating like hell, being so afraid. For all he knew, those fools could have flipped out, clapped and stabbed him up. The manager shut his eyelids briefly and swallowed the ball of nervousness in his throat. *Oh, please God… don't let one of these hoodlums kill me*, he thought.

"Looks like the bell has rung, so recess is over. I guess we'll play some other time."

Pain lowered his banger, stashing it inside of his waistline.

"Make sho' you bring yo' Big Wheel next time, ol' sucka duck ass nigga."

Blessyn let the steak knife drop from his hand. It clinked on the broken glass and loose silverware when it struck the floor. While the two men were popping shit at one another, Treasure was pulling her check book out of her purse and scribbling down numbers. Right after, she ripped the check free from the book and passed it to the manager. She spoke to him as he looked over the digits she had written down.

"Look, I'm sorry about all of this. I've written down enough to pay for damages. I also threw in enough to pay for everyone's meal and a bottle of whatever champagne they'd like. I trust this won't hit the news or airwaves."

She looked him square in the eyes and waited for his confirmation. He nodded yes.

"As for myself and my staff, we won't say a word, and if any of the patrons here say anything, we'll completely deny it."

He folded up the check and shoved it inside of his slacks.

"Oh thank you, thank you, thank you," Treasure told him repeatedly, hands together like she was praying. He smiled and nodded. Treasure and Skylar looked all around them, and sure enough, all eyes were on them.

"Come on, bro bro."

Skylar grabbed Pain's hand and headed toward the exit.

"We've gotta get outta here, 'fore the Rollers show up."

"Let's go."

Blessyn grabbed Treasure's hand and headed for the exit as well. Treasure and Skylar locked eyes. Skylar made her hand into the shape of a telephone and placed it to her ear, mouthing to her 'call me.' The Princess of R&B nodded. She then looked up to Pain, who was focused on Blessyn. Right then, he looked back at her. Their eyes lingered on one another, a million thoughts shooting through their brains, but neither one of them knowing what to say. As soon as they crossed the threshold into the night's air, they departed and went to their respective vehicles.

Skylar grabbed the keys from Pain to his Cutlass and jumped behind the wheel. As soon as she cranked that son of a bitch up, E-40's "Captain Save-A-Hoe" exploded from the speakers, flooding the interior. She shifted the gears and was about to pull off when she looked to her brother. She found him rummaging through his glove box, spilling all kinds of loose papers onto the floor. When he found what he was looking for, he told her that he would be right back and hopped out of the Hood Classic. When he slammed the door shut and went stalking down the sidewalk, Skylar looked over her shoulder through the back window.

God, please don't let my brotha pop this old gangbanging ass nigga out here, she thought to herself.

CHAPTER EIGHT

Treasure and Blessyn hopped inside of his Lambo, shutting the doors one after another.

"Ol' punk ass nigga... I should have gave him the business," Blessyn said to no one in particular, activating his stash box. When it opened, he took out his ratchet and chambered a round in its head. A knock at the passenger side window startled him, and he pointed his weapon at it. There, he found Pain hunched over in the tinted window, eyes focused on Treasure. He knew there was a gun on him, not because he could see it but because he could feel it. He didn't care though. Nah, his lady held his undivided attention.

"Remember this...remember us."

He sat the picture strip into the opening of the window. He then pressed his middle finger against the window's glass. That 'fuck you' was for Blessyn. The insult left him fuming, eyebrows arched and nostrils flaring. He wanted to jump out on Pain and do him dirty with his gun, but he knew that if he slumped him, he'd be the number one suspect. As he fired up the Lamborghini and pulled off, Treasure let the window down and snatched the picture strip.

The night was cool, and well-lit, thanks to the rides of the carnival. Children and adults laughter and conversations filled the air. The playful music coming from the rides set the tone for the participants of festival. The announcers' voices blared through their blow horns as they tried to bait patrons to play their games. People were coming and going. Some were on lines to get on rides, to purchase food, to turn in tickets to pick the item that they won, or to see a show. Everyone seemed to be in their own little world, oblivious to what everyone else was doing. This went especially for Pain and Treasure.

Treasure stood beside Pain with his leather jacket wrapped around her shoulders. She ate cotton candy as she watched her man throw balls at the mechanism that would drop the dude sitting on the bench above the water of the tank. An hour and fifty balls later, the thug found himself in his wife beater and shiny from sweat. His arm was aching like hell having thrown so many balls, but the stubborn bastard refused to leave the carnival without his girl having the huge stuffed pink and red bunny rabbit that she desired.

Ping! Dink! Cling! Ring!

The balls deflected off of the mechanism, not strong enough to knock the damn thing down. Pain threw the last ball, and it missed the mechanism entirely, nearly striking a passerby in the side of the head. The nigga turned around scowling, feeling the air from the ball flying by his ear. He looked like he was ready to get it popping, but Pain wasn't studying him. He was nice with them hands and those guns. However homie wanted to handle it wasn't a thing, but he wasn't there on no bullshit that night. Nah, he was there with his girl, trying to show her a good time, so he'd put his gangsta on the shelf for the time being.

"My bad, G!" Pain called out to dude he nearly hit with the last ball thrown. He then rapidly counted off ten one-dollar bills and passed them to the short portly man in suspenders and wicker hat that was running the show.

"You worried about him. You need to be worrying about me, 'cause you lookin' bad out here, little man. You haven't—"

Boom!

The ball struck the mechanism on the bullseye, knocking it down. Before the smart mouthed nigga on the bench could say anything else, his ass was splashing down in the tank of water, splashing water everywhere.

"Yeah, mothafucka. That's game!" Pain called out victoriously.

"Whoooo, yeah! My baby did it!" Treasure jumped up and down, clapping her hands. Pain picked the stuffed bunny she wanted, and the man in the wicker hat handed it to her. Excited, she kissed her man hard and smacked him on the ass like a basketball player would his opponent on the opposite team.

"Good job, handsome. Can you hold it for me though?"

He nodded yes and took the rabbit. Hand and hand, they strolled through the carnival looking around. She bought a funnel cake, eating some and feeding her man some as well.

"Hey, you wanna take some pictures with me?" she asked with one jaw full, still snacking on the funnel cake.

"Uhhh, I don't know, love. I ain't never been one for flicks," Pain said, hoping not to disappoint her.

"Awww, pretty please," Treasure tilted her head down and pouted her lip, batting her eyelashes. She made a sad ass puppy dog face, and he couldn't help but laugh and agree.

"Aww, all right."

"Okay... thanks, baby."

She smiled and gave him a quick peck on the lips. Next, she stuffed her face with the last of the cake and sucked the glaze from off of her fingers and thumb. Afterwards, she wiped her hands with the napkins and grabbed her boo's hand, hurrying toward the picture booth. Treasure drew the curtain of the booth back and took the stuffed bunny from Pain, sitting it down. Once he sat on the seat inside, she climbed in and sat on his lap, dropping quarters into the slot.

"Alright... gotta make sure we're looking good and shit. Can't have these bum ass niggas or these dusty ass hoes hating on the king and queen, yah mean?"

Hurriedly, Treasure fixed her hair and fluffed out Pain's beard with her hands. She smiled as she did this, looking into his light brown eyes. They looked like cinnamon Cheerios set against his dark caramel complexion. Suddenly, Pain cracked a smile of his own, staring into the beautiful face of the woman occupying his lap. The two of them seemed to be holding one another's gaze for a lifetime, and then it happened. He said the magic words.

"I love you, Treasure."

At that precise moment, the camera inside of the booth began snapping. It captured Treasure's surprised expression and then the look on her face when she told him that she loved him too. He placed his hand behind her neck, and she slid her hands behind his, pulling him closer. They kissed slowly, then slightly sped up, eyes closed. They moved their mouths like they were making love with their mouths. The entire time, the camera was going off, snapping these still images for them to remember for an eternity.

Treasure stared down at the picture strip with a smile stretched across her face. Her eyes became teary thinking back to that night. It was the same night that she and Pain had told each other that they loved one another. It was also the same night that they made passionate love. Their first time wasn't awkward at all. It was like the universe had planned it for eons, and it went down exactly how it was orchestrated. It was from that and how they got along that they knew they were meant to be together for the rest of their lives.

Water slowly outlined the rim of Treasure's eyes. The first teardrop went to fall from her right eye, and she swiped it away with her fingers and thumb. She sniffled, finding herself reliving that moment in time. Unbeknownst to her, Blessyn was pissed the fuck off. His maddened face snapped from the windshield to her. At this time, the street lights were flashing on and off of them as the Lamborghini sped through the streets. Their windows were partially cracked, so the occasional breeze blew inside, disturbing the loose hairs on their heads and clothing. Blessyn seemed to be getting madder and madder as he looked back and forth between Treasure and the windshield. As the light flashed on and off of their faces, he seemed to become angrier.

Suddenly, Blessyn snatched the picture strip from the R&B diva's hand, pulling her back to this decade. She seemed to come alive a second time, realizing where the hell she was. Blessyn let his window all the way down. Seeing this, Treasure's eyes grew big because she knew what he was about to do. She tried reaching for the picture strip, but he shrugged her off. By then, it was already too late. The nigga had tossed the picture strip out of the window.

"You got me fucked up, thinking you gone be boo hooin' ova the next nigga in my mothafuckin' ride! Not me! Not I! Not Blessyn!"

"Noooooooooooo!" Treasure bellowed, tears sliding down her cheeks. She started swinging on his ass, catching him in his head and shoulder. He tried his best to bob and weave her attack, but he was still catching those blows.

"Stop! Stop 'fore you make me wreck this mothafucka, blood!"

He swerved from left to right, trying not to hit cars in other lanes. The vehicles that were almost struck horns were blown, and their drivers hollered insults out of their windows. Blessyn swept past several lanes until he reached the shoulder of the freeway. Throwing the Lambo in park, he removed the keys and jumped out. He rounded the car heatedly and snatched open the front passenger side door, pulling Treasure's ass out kicking and screaming. Having tossed her to the ground, he tossed out her purse and let the door down. Next, he was running back around to the driver side and jumping in.

The purple vehicle sped off, leaving dust up in its wake. Treasure grabbed her purse and scrambled to her feet. She pulled out some Kleenex and dabbed her tearing eyes as she walked down the shoulder of the freeway. Passing cars tried to pick her up, but she ignored them, continuing her trek along the side of the road.

Treasure was hurt that Blessyn had thrown away that picture strip of her and Pain. It was something that she could never replace, and it was priceless as far as she was concerned. If she was lucky, some good Samaritan would find it, look her up, and mail it back to her. The chances weren't likely though. Not many people in the world were willing to go out of their way for the people they knew, let alone the people they didn't know. Hearing a vehicle beside her, Treasure looked and found Blessyn's Lamborghini. Immediately, she snapped her head forward and looked ahead, turning her nose up at him. This was her way of giving him her ass to kiss for him kicking her out of his ride.

The front passenger side window descended, and Blessyn's head appeared in the window. He coasted alongside her, waiting for her to look his way so that he could holler at her, but she never did. That's when he went ahead to speak to her.

"Look, I shouldn't have thrown you outta my ride like that, but you know you were dead ass wrong for gettin' all emotional and shit like that in front of me behind anotha nigga. I mean, let that had of been me actin' like that behind some chicken head. You couldn't tell me you wouldn't have thrown one of yo' famous ghetto girl tantrums."

Having spoken his peace, he continued to ride along beside her, waiting for her response. Treasure knew that Blessyn was right. Although she didn't love the nigga, she did like his old gangsta ass. She knew that she would have showed her natural black ass had some bitch had him like she was behind that picture strip like Pain had her. Still, she was in her feelings, so she was gone make Blessyn's ass work just that much harder for her understanding and forgiveness.

Seeing that he was getting nowhere fast, Blessyn, the crazy mothafucka that he is, parked his $200,000 dollar sports car on the shoulder of the freeway and hopped out to pursue his woman. He walked along beside her, shooting major cap until he got her to agree to come home with him.

****

Skylar drove her brother's Cutlass through the streets, nodding her head to one of Treasure's songs that just so happened to come on the radio. Pain, on the other hand, was lying back in the front passenger seat, twisting up a blunt for them to smoke. Skylar couldn't help glancing back and forth between the windshield and her brother. She knew that he was with the shit, but to pop that nigga, Blessyn, in a restaurant would have been stupid as hell. There wouldn't have been any way that he could have beaten that murder rap.

"Yo, bro bro," Skylar glanced over at him.

"'Sup, sis?" he responded, focusing on the blunt as he prepared it.

"You wild… I mean real wild… for real."

She cracked a grin. He slightly frowned and said, "What chu mean?"

"Yo, was you seriously about to give that nigga, Blessyn, the B.I up in there?" she questioned, hoping that he'd say no.

"Fucking right! Fuck that nigga."

He took the time to lick the bleezy shut.

"All gangstas don't flag red and blue."

He swept the flame of the lighter back and forth beneath the blunt, sealing it shut. Afterwards, he took his the time to take a couple of puffs, polluting the air.

"You still love her, don't chu?" she asked, taking the bleezy from his pinched fingers.

"Ahhh, fuck!" he shouted in pain, brows furrowed.

"What's wrong?" a frowning Skylar looked from the windshield to her brother, wondering what the fuck was going on.

"I felt…I felt like needles stabbing me in my chest…repeatedly."

He looked under his shirt, and nothing was there. He felt on his chest, but there weren't any wounds or blood there. He let his shirt fall back down over him and relaxed a little.

"You good?"

"Yeah, I'm straight. I don't know what the fuck I just felt, but that's weird."

"You gone have to get that checked out… seriously."

"I will, but, uh yeah… I don't know what I'ma do, but I gotta get Treasure back, bird. She is the love of my life, yah mean? Can't nobody tell me that God didn't make that girl especially for me."

Pain spoke the words that his heart felt. From the look in his eyes, his sister could tell that he was being completely honest.

"Don't worry, bro bro. Things will work themselves out," she said, holding smoke in her lungs.

"Things will work themselves out."

She blew out smoke and passed the bleezy back to him. He took it and nodded in agreeance, looking out of the passenger side window as he sucked on the end of the blunt.

Later that night…

Treasure lay in bed beside Blessyn who was asleep, snoring like a hog. The lights were out, and blue illumination from the outside light shining through the window's blinds shone on their forms. Treasure lay in bed, staring up at the ceiling, thinking about that nigga, Pain. She wished she would have just said fuck it and went home with him, but she let Blessyn's smooth talking ass coerce her into going back to his place. Although he cracked for the pussy, she played him to the left. There wasn't any way in hell she was about to let him run dick up in her that night. Her mind was too occupied with thoughts of Pain.

No matter how hard she tried to shake his old thug ass from out of her head, he hung on. She still wanted him. She still needed him, so she hoped things would all come together so they could get back together again. Truthfully, she wanted to call and tell him then that she was willing to give them another shot, but she had to make him sweat it out just a little longer. Although she loved him with all of her heart, she knew that she'd lose his respect if she were to allow him back in her life so soon.

Hearing her cellular vibrate and light up the inside of her jean pocket, Treasure scooped them up and pulled the device out. Looking at the screen, she saw that it was her girl, Skylar, and a smile stretched across her face. She hadn't spoken to her in a couple of days, so she was glad that she'd called like she said she would.

"What's up baaaaatch?" Treasure answered playfully, in a hushed tone.

"Nothing, baaaaatch," Skylar replied playfully, laughing afterwards.

"You made it home safe?" she asked on a serious note. Treasure looked at Blessyn and wondered if she should lie or tell her best friend the truth.

"Nah. I'm at this nigga, Blessyn's, spot."

"Oh really?" she said amusingly, implying to her that she and Blessyn were fucking that night.

"Ain't nothing go down between me and this old crazy ass nigga."

She took the time to look at her French tipped nails.

"Nah, real shit… he was try'na fuck, but I just let him eat me my pussy. Hell, I shouldn't have even let it go that far. I told you how this nigga been in his feelings and shit lately."

Treasure looked over at Blessyn, and he was hanging halfway out of the bed, snoring even louder.

"Yeah, I remember."

There was silence for a minute, and then Treasure spoke again.

"Yo, Sky…you know you my bitch, right?"

"Foreva and a day."

"That shit between Trip and Blessyn…"

"Don't even wet that shit, boo. That's between them, but if he hurts my brotha, you know all bets are off, right?"

"Right… and I'ma be right there witchu, holding it down. You know don't no nigga come before us."

"That's my A-one."

"Since Day-one."

"Tadowl."

"Who you talkin' to, baby?" Treasure heard some nigga in the background.

"Treasure, nigga…. why you so nosey?"

"I know you ain't talkin'. Tell lil' mama I said what's up."

"You hear this nigga, Tee?" Skylar asked Treasure.

"Yeah, tell my nigga, Tank, I said what's good with it?"

"She said what's good?"

"Lemme see the jack," Treasure heard him drawing closer, and then he came on the phone.

"Ain't shit… just finna run up in yo' home girl and have her scaling these walls like Spider Man or some shit."

"Hahahahaha! T.M.I, nigga."

"My fault."

"Gimme the phone, nigga."

She heard Skylar snatch the phone from her dude.

"Aye, girl. Lemme call you back. You know how this fool ass nigga of mine acts when he don't get his medicine."

While she was talking, Tank's short buff neck ass was pulling off of her clothes. The last thing to go was her thong.

He threw them bitches across the room and left her butt naked with a fat wet pussy. He then positioned her so that her teardrop ass would be tooted up in the air, just like his old rough neck ass liked it.

"All right, girl. Gone and—"

"Yo, sis… she gone have to call you back, alright?" Tank said, stroking his thick, veined dick while Skylar kneeled down to him and started sucking on his long, wrinkled nut sack. His eyelids were shut and he was licking his lips, enjoying the pleasure that was being bestowed upon him.

"Okay. Y'all make sure y'all wrap it up. I'm too young to be an auntie now," she smiled.

"I got chu faded. Peace."

He disconnected the call. Treasure stashed her cell phone inside of her bag and cautiously got dressed, making sure she didn't wake Blessyn's ass up. The last thing she grabbed was her bag and her shoes which she didn't even bother to slip on. She tiptoed her ass to the door in a hurry and pulled it open. She was just walking through it when she stopped and turned around to Blessyn. Standing there, she stared at him, listening to him snore as she took a deep breath. *When I finally call this thing off, I just know this nigga is not gonna take it well*, she thought to herself.

Treasure allowed her eyes to linger on Blessyn for a while longer before making her exit. When the time came for her to give him the boot, she hoped that he took it well, but something at the back of her mind told her he wouldn't.

CHAPTER NINE

Having just gotten out of the shower and wrapped a towel around his waist, Pain stood before the medicine cabinet's fogged mirror. Taking his hand, he wiped a circle in the mirror, revealing a part of him with each circular motion. Soon, he found his reflection staring back at him, his beard dripping wet. He turned his head from left to right to get a good look at himself as he held his chin. A smile stretched across his full lips, showcasing his teeth. Picking up his natural fork with the Black power fist from off of the sink, he went on to pick out his nappy facial hair. Once he was done picking out his beard, he sat the natural fork back down on the sink. Gripping the sink on either side, he leaned forward, studying his appearance. It was then that he noticed all of the wounds that covered his body and arms. First, there was the old scars he'd gotten from being shot eleven times, and then there was the old nasty slashes he'd been rewarded for cheating. Instantly, his ex-girlfriend, Treasure, came to mind. He had really fucked up when he lost her. There wasn't any doubt in his mind that little mama was *the one*. She was everything that he wanted in a woman and then some. No one was perfect, but she was definitely perfect for him.

Six months ago, Pain and Treasure's relationship had been going through a rough patch, being that she was always on the road doing shows and shit. Although she kept in contact with him through Skype, texting, and phone calls, it paled in comparison to her being there beside him. Treasure had been gone almost six months, and he had become sexual frustrated. Sure… phone sex was cool, but nothing beat out the feeling of being inside of some warm wet pussy. Even with the urge to satisfy his sexual hunger being intensely strong, the thug was able to shake off his needs.

As the days were winding down, it was getting harder and harder, especially with Treasure's cousin, Fiona, coming on to him. Treasure had agreed to let her stay at their condo until she got back on her feet. This was a big mistake, because little mama was a thirst trap that was dying to have her cousin's man run up in her. She'd wanted to have that nigga, Pain, since the first time she laid eyes on him at Treasure's birthday party down in Miami. She'd pulled out every trick that was in her bag, but homie was biting for the bait that she was trying to hook him with. He was just too loyal and faithful to her big cousin.

When Pain told Treasure about her relative pushing up on him, she pressed her at her party, and Fiona apologized to her. She hit her with some bullshit about her being drunk and high out of her mind, and not realizing that it was Pain until she began to sober up. The princess of R&B took her word for it and went back to her party, while Fiona started plotting on another way to get her man to come up off of that dick. A few months later, she made up a story about her getting evicted from her apartment and needing a place to hold up. Being that old girl was family, Treasure allowed her to kick up her heels, going against her better judgment.

Fiona wore skimpy clothing that showed off all of the body that her mother had gifted her with. She threw a little something in her walk when she knew Pain was watching her, and she could tell that his defenses were beginning to wear thin. One night, she decided to make her move on him while he was chilling in the living room, watching Netflix and taking a bleezy to the head.

Pain was slumped down on the couch, high out of his fucking mind. He was bare chested, and all of his tattoos were on display. His brown Dickies hung below his waist, and his feet were inside a pair of Corduroy house shoes. The blue illumination from the flat-screen TV flickered on his face as he leaned forward and mashed out what was left of his blunt. His twisting and turning of the blunt inside of the ashtray left black streaks at the bottom of it. He was just about to lean back on the couch when he saw something stirring around in the darkness, causing him to narrow his eyelids to get a better look. Thinking that it was better to be safe than sorry, he snatched his hammer off of the side of him where it was lying. He'd just pressed the safety button on his weapon and was about to get off, when what he saw next surprised the hell out of him. Fiona came sashaying out of the shadows as naked as the day that she was born. Her wide hips rocked back and forth with each step that she took, her ample breast bouncing gently. Her log curly hair dangled before her eyes, distorting the image of her face and giving her a dangerous look. The sexy ghetto goddess licked her lips, appearing as if she was ready to eat him alive.

Pain's eyes widened, and his lips peeled apart, seeing her fine ass sauntering in his direction. He took her in from head to toe. This caused the meat in his pants to grow solid and nudge at his zipper.

"Fee, don't chu think you should put on some—"

Before he could finish, she was already straddling his lap and snatching his gun from out of his hand, sitting it aside on the couch. She threw her arms around his neck and mashed her soft lips against his. Little mama stuck her tongue inside of his mouth and angled her head, kissing him hard and lustfully.

He tried to pull her arms from around his neck and turn his head, but she held him in place. Eventually, he fell weak, engaging in the act of cheating with his girl's cousin. There were heavy breaths and saliva sloshing around in their mouths as they kissed. While their lips were busy, she moved her hands down to his belt and unbuckled it. Once she pulled it loose from its loops, she threw it aside. She pulled on his bottom lip gently and then kissed him, before slithering her naked ass down his torso. She pulled his boxers down and met a nest of nappy hair that lead down to a thick penis with veins running throughout it. She took it into her mouth and slurped him up, moving her head up and down. He sat up on the couch and stared down at her with a balled up face. He hated and loved her at the same time for blessing him with some wicked head and causing him to fall to her mercy.

"Mmmmm hmmmm."

Fiona made sexual noises as she stared up at Pain, watching his eyelids flicker white. His eyes were rolled to the back of his head, and his lips were trembling. Her lips slightly curled at the end, pleased that she was bringing her cousin's man to sexual bliss. He squirmed where he was perched, running his fingers through her dookie braided hair. It got so good to him that he slowly began to hump her mouth, causing her to gag.

"Gaaggggg!"

Tears filled her eyes and ran down her cheeks. Saliva built up in her grill. Veins formed at her temples and up her neck. That nigga, Pain, was fucking her mouth intensely.

"Ol' nasty bitch… keep tempting a nigga… throwing the pussy at me!" *he said through gritted teeth and stared down at her. His tattooed hand held the back of her skull as he jabbed* her mouth. His dick was glistening, being that her slopping grill was juicy.

"Is this what chu won't? Huh? Is it?"

His tongue hung out the side of his lips, and he thrust hard and fast. He was fucking her face like he was trying to hurt it bad.

"Uhhhhh, here we go," he croaked, throwing his head back and shutting his eyelids briefly. When he brought his chin down, he gripped home girl's head with both hands.

"Oooooh, yeah! I'm 'bouta bust right in yo' mothafucking mouth! Unh! Unh!" he continued his pummeling of her mouth, making saliva ooze out of her mouth. Her warm saliva spilled out on to his nappy pubic hair, causing it to glisten.

"Raahhhh!" he hollered aloud and made an ugly face, unleashing all of that warm, creamy semen down into her throat. He slumped where he was after busting a nut, watching her continue to suck him off through narrowed eyelids. She pulled her head back slowly, revealing the length of his dick inch by inch. She did this until his grown man was free of her lips. Afterwards, he held her mouth open to showcase his jizz cupped in her tongue. Looking him dead in the eyes, she swallowed and sucked on her fingers as if they were stained with chocolate.

Pain looked above Fiona's head and saw a silhouette standing in the doorway of the hallway. He narrowed his eyelids just that much further, and that's when he noticed that it was Treasure. She was dressed in a trench coat and wearing a black teddy beneath it with matching high heeled shoes. Acknowledging this, his eyes grew huge, and he gasped. Fiona wiped her mouth with the back of her fist and whipped her head around too. She saw Treasure there as well. Tears welled up in the R&B superstar's eyes.

"I...I caught an earlier flight home," her voice cracked under her raw emotions. She was devastated to have walked in on her man and her cousin fucking around.

"I...I thought I'd surprise you since your birthday is tomorrow."

She shut her eyelids, and tears shot down her cheeks. Right after, she sniffled and swallowed the ball of hurt that had formed in her throat.

"Baby, lemme explain..."

Pain jumped to his feet and tucked his dick back inside of his boxers, zipping up his Dickie shorts. Fiona snatched a pillow from off of the couch to hide her nakedness behind. Treasure's eyelids snapped open, and her face balled up tight.

"Ain't nothing to explain, Trip. I walked in on my favorite cousin sucking my man's dick. I know exactly what's going on here. You not only disrespected me, but you disrespected my house! Both of you bitches dead!"

She swayed her manicured finger between the two of them and took off running in the direction of the kitchen, ducking off inside. In a blink of an eye, she was running out of that bitch with two butcher knives in her fists, ready to cut their trifling asses every way but loose.

"Oooh shit!"

Pain's eyelids snapped open, and he threw up his arm as his boo brought the butcher's knife down. The blade pierced his flesh and went half way through his arm, blood specs clung to her face. She looked like a woman gone mad. Fire danced in her pupils, and her nostrils were pulsating as she continued to stab that ass up. Once he fell to the floor, cradling his bleeding arms, Treasure set her sights on her cousin, Fiona. Her fucking heart damn near exploded in her chest seeing the madness in her relative's eyes.

"Cuz, it ain't even—" she was cut short by the animalistic growl of Treasure as she went charging at her, crimson stained butcher knives in both of her fists. Fiona hauled ass out of the living room with Treasure taking swipes at her back, sending blood everywhere. The bitch stopped at the front door to unlock it, and the diva was still slicing away at her back. She winced, feeling her flesh behind split open. Her back burned like it was on fire, and tears twinkled in her eyes. She hollered out like a wounded animal as she tried her best to hurry up and unlock the locks of the doors.

"Ah! Ahh! Ahhh! Ahhhh!"

Fiona threw her head back further and further, feeling the flames that the knives created as they sliced at her back. Tears flew down her cheeks. She had just taken the chain from across the door and pulled it open when Treasure brought one of the butcher's knives down on her shoulder. The R&B superstar squeezed her eyelids shut just as her victim's blood speckled her face. Fiona screamed so loud from the brutal assault that she could have awoken the deaf. Out of reflex, she kicked her cousin in her mid-section and sent her flying back inside of her baby mansion, crashing to the floor and grimacing. The impact sent her knives spinning around in circles across the floor. One disappeared beneath the living room couch where Pain was moaning in agony while the other bumped up against the leg of her white Grand Piano.

Angrier than she was before, Treasure scrambled to her feet and snatched up the knife that had bumped up against the leg of the piano. When she turned back around, she saw her cousin's minced, bloody back as she made hurried footsteps off the grounds of her mansion. Treasure was out of the door crying, slobbering, and hurling profanities at her victim. She held her knife back above her shoulder as she chased her hoe ass up the block. Fiona screamed out for help and constantly looked over her shoulder to see if her assailant was still on her. Not only was she still on her, she wasn't too far behind.

"Hellllllp! Somebody, pleeeeease hellllllp me," Fiona screamed at the top of her lungs. She ran down the street butt naked, ass and titties jiggling along the way. Her head was on a swivel, looking all around for someplace to take solace or someone that would help her. She continued to scream aloud. Suddenly, the porch lights of the surrounding homes in the neighborhood began to come on in a domino effect.

The residents began stepping out onto their porches to see what the hell was going on. At the same time that this was going on, police car sirens filled the air. They weren't far behind. Their red and blue lights shining on Fiona and Treasure's faces made this apparent.

"You dirty ass, scandalous skeeza! You fuck my man inside of my house, and I gave yo' old hoe ass a place to stay? I'ma kill you, bitch. I swear on my mama's grave, I'ma murder yo' ass!"

Treasure clenched her jaws so tightly that her skeletal bone structure shown in them. Her eyes were red webbed and glassy. She'd definitely snapped after seeing her boo getting his dick sucked by her hoe ass cousin.

Pain staggered out of the baby mansion and bumped up against one of the pillars on the porch, cradling his bleeding arms. His chest and stomach were smeared in blood, and agony was across his face. The nigga was leaking on the porch and starting to feel woozy due to his loss of blood. He looked up the block and saw his lady chasing after her cousin with a goddamn butcher's knife. He was breathing heavily, and his chest was jumping rapidly, terrified of what she may do.

"Treaaaasureeeeeeeee!" Pain called out to his woman as loud as he could, nearly going hoarse. It didn't matter though. She didn't hear his ass. Fuck no... she had zoned the fuck out, and the only thing she was focused on was killing Fiona's punk ass.

Urrrrrrrrk! Urrrrrrrk!

Two police cars came swinging into a stop beside the curb. Just as police officers were hopping out of their vehicles and reaching for their holstered weapons, Fiona was running out into the street for them. One of them grabbed her by the arm and pulled her behind him. She watched over his shoulder as he and the other officers drew down on a crazed Treasure, stopping her dead in her tracks. Treasure froze where she was with her butcher's knife held over her shoulder, dripping blood from its tip. Her head snapped around to all of the pigs that had their guns pointed at her, tears constantly sliding down her face. The red and blue lights continued to shine in her face as she took in all of the hostile faces of the men that held her at gunpoint.

Treasure had this look in her eyes, like she was trying to decide whether she was going to try her luck against the police officer's bullets. Seeing this, Pain came running off of the mansion's grounds.

"Baby, drop the knife. Drop it right now!"

Pain came running toward the love of his life.

"Drop your weapon! Drop your goddamn weapon now!" the officers sounded off in unison. Treasure's head snapped around to all of the scowling faces of the trigger happy police men. She held her butcher's knife in place as tears flooded her cheeks, looking around frantically. She kept hearing her man's voice over and over again, chanting to her to drop her knife. His voice went from normal to sounding like it had been chopped and screwed. Finally, she dropped the knife, and it clasped to the asphalt. Dropping to her knees, she smacked her hands over her face and balled her eyes out until the police moved in to cuff her black ass up.

Pain and Fiona were loaded into the back of ambulances, and Treasure was taken down to the precinct and booked. Her charges were put to bed, being that Showtime had gotten into contact with the right people and put the right money into the right hands. The CEO of Big Willie records made it so that it seemed like nothing had occurred that night. Treasure was let out that very night and whisked home in a limousine that he'd sent for her. The next couple of days, Pain had been trying to get in touch with her, but she curved all of his calls. Depressed, all she did was sulk and lay in bed.

Pain stood before the medicine cabinet's mirror, touching his old knife wounds. His eyes were so fixated on his reflection that he didn't hear the knocks at his door. The knocking grew louder and louder until he eventually snapped out of his spellbound state

Knock! Knock! Knock!

"Who is it?" Pain called out, turning his head away from the medicine cabinet's mirror. He had just came back from the night Treasure had sliced his ass up.

Knock! Knock! Knock!

Pain picked up his forty-five automatic handgun from off of the sink. Adjusting his towel around his waist, he walked out of the bathroom dropping droplets of water on the tiled floor. The knocking continued as he approached. He was tight lipped though, because if the wrong mothafucka was behind the door, he was going to get some act-right. Pain took a peek through the peephole of the door of his home. His demeanor changed when he saw who it was at his door, lowering his ratchet to his side. He unchained and unlocked the door, pulling it open. On his doorstep, he found Epic and Lil' Joe. Epic looked mad ass fuck while Lil' Joe looked kind of high to him. The meat of Pain's brows mushed together, forming a bridge. His mind wandered as his head snapped back and forth between his homies.

"Who died?"

CHAPTER TEN

"We got hit," Epic told Pain. Pain's forehead wrinkled, and he responded.

"Fuck you talking about?"

"Some bloods jacked me and Lil' Joe for the shipment."

Pain grabbed him by the front of his shirt and forced him up against the wall so hard that his snapback fell off of his head from the impact, landing on the floor beside his sneaker.

"My nigga, you betta be playing with me right now."

"I really wish I fuckin' was, but I'm not!"

Epic pushed him from off his off of his person and snatched up his snapback, adjusting it on his head.

"We got hit. Now, we peeped the move and got it poppin' with 'em, but they ended up layin' that nigga, Manny, down."

Pain's head snapped to Lil' Joe and he said, while pointing to Epic, "Is this fool serious, man?"

"Yeah, Pain… that's how it went down," Lil' Joe confirmed, looking him dead in his eyes. He lied with a straight face, but with glassy eyes. He knew that he was in a world of shit, because the nigga that Epic offed was connected to the Forty Thieves crew. They were supposed to be some of the most ruthless criminals assembled. They robbed, stole, killed, extorted and acted as hired hands. It was said that these men were the bastard muscles from an infamous drug czar over in Mexico. Once the drug lord had gotten taken out by the task force across the border, the collective was left to fend for themselves.

"Fuck! Fuck! Fuck! Fuck!"

The punches he threw at the wall in a fit of rage came back to back, denting a hole in the wall. With each blow that landed, the hole in the wall grew larger and larger. Afterwards, he pressed his palms against the wall and took a deep breath, trying to calm himself down as best as he could. Shutting his eyelids briefly, he finally pulled himself together.

"We've got ourselves a situation here. Once their people find out that Manny was murdered and their product is gone, they're immediately gonna think we had something to do with it, no matter what the fuck we say."

"Me and Lil' Joe were just saying that," Epic informed him.

"That's why after we catch up with these fools that took us for the blocks, we gone smash them lil' mothafuckas, too."

"Yo, chill out on all of that kinda talk, E. We don't wanna go to war with these people unless we have to."

Pain picked up his telephone and speed dialed the top dawg of the Forty Thieves. He placed his finger to his lips as he listened to the telephone ring. Epic and Lil' Joe exchanged glances.

****

Bud sat before a canvas before with his oils by his side, tongue hanging out of the side of his mouth. With each stroke of his brush, he was creating his latest piece. Bud was a five-foot-nine white dude. His hair was dyed blonde, but the natural growth of his brunette hair had begun to show at his roots. His brow was pierced, and he had plugs in his ears the size of bottle caps. He wore an ugly Hawaiian shirt that was open to his wife beater which he wore underneath it and stonewashed blue jeans, all of which were smeared with an array of the colorful paints he'd been using.

The walls of Bud's studio apartment were covered with portraits he'd painted himself. The hardwood floor of the unit was absent of furniture, save for the worn sofa and the milk-crate supporting an old twenty-inch television set.

There was a knock at the door that startled Bud. He put his paint brush down and crept toward the door, shuffling toward it in his beat up Nikes. The knocks at the door continued as he looked through the peephole, paint stained hands placed on either side of the door. Seeing who it was, his eyes bulged, and he gasped fearfully. It was then that he bolted toward the window and slid it open, letting a cool breeze inside of his studio apartment. As he brought his scrawny leg over the window seal, someone shoved a banger into his face, mashing it against his big ass nose. His eyelids stretched open, and his hands shot up in surrender, trembling. Slowly, he brought his foot back inside of the apartment and a four-foot man wearing a ski-mask along with it.

Boom!

The front door flew open, sending a spray of splinters and debris everywhere. A shaved-head Mexican man wearing a hood, black sunglasses, and a neoprene mask over the lower half of his face came strolling inside of the unit, lugging along an AK-47. His eyes were menacing, and his demeanor was threatening. When Bud saw this short, big headed mothafucka coming in his direction, the color drained from his face instantly. Feeling his bladder growing hot, he looked down to see if he was about to piss on himself. When he saw that he wasn't, he looked back up just in time to get the butt of the intruder's AK slammed into the side of his face, fracturing his cheekbone and sending him hurling toward the floor.

Bud found himself lying at shaved-head's feet, moaning in pain, holding the side of his face. He attempted to get upon his feet several times, but he kept falling down like a calf that had just been birthed.

"I know you heard me at the door, puto," shaved-head barked.

"You tried to climb down the fire escape when you heard me coming, didn't you?"

"I wasn't trying to run from you, Premo. I swear to God, bro!" Bud lied, looking up at his attacker sadly and holding the side of his swelling face.

"I was just opening the window to let some fresh air in is all."

Premo looked to the shorter masked man, and he shook his head. This let him know that Bud's junky ass was lying. He scowled and kicked Bud in his stomach hard as fuck, knocking the wind out of the son of a bitch.

"Lying sack of shit," he barked on him, pulling up a chair and sitting down beside his prey. He then leaned over to him and said, "Where's the fedia, homes?"

A few years ago, Bud had been busted on a B.N.E charge and sent straight to Corcoran State Penitentiary. As soon as he hit the yard, he was being bullied and harassed. In fear for his life, not to mention ill from not having a shot of dope for the past few days, he turned to someone that put him in touch with an underworld figure that could help him.

The underworld figure was known as Desmond, the head honcho of the Forty Thieves crew. He had twelve of his home boys behind the wall. This was more than enough muscle to keep Bud's lily white ass in one piece. Desmond offered him protection as well as dope during his stretch, for a fee of course. Seeing no other choice in the matter, Bud agreed to the deal and shook hands with the devil himself. His parents paid the wages it would take to keep their boy safe, but during the last year of Bud's bid they went broke.

Month after month, they promised to pay Desmond, and he kept his vale of protection over Bud. When it started to look like he would never get the money he was promised, Desmond had the men he had inside turn their shanks on Bud. Bud managed to get away with a few minor wounds, so the Lord was indeed looking out for his pale ass. Seeing no other choice, that nigga Bud rolled up his shit and entered protective custody. He stayed there for the rest of his stretch.

Bud was twenty grand in debt when he was paroled. He ducked and dodged Desmond's people for as long as he could, making payments here and there with the money he made selling his paintings, but a couple of hundred bucks every so often just wasn't enough. The top dawg wanted his all in one shot.

"I…I…" Bud stuttered, quivering from terror.

"I what, mothafucka!" he screamed on him.

"I have some of it," Bud told him and swallowed the lump of fear that had formed in his throat.

"It's in the coffee canister in the cupboard."

"Skrappy."

Premo looked to the shorter man, and he headed toward the kitchen. A moment later, he returned with a knot of bills which he forked over to the top dawg. Bullet popped the rubber-band that held the bills together and quickly thumbed through them, one by one. There were three $100 dollar bills and $200 dollars in singles.

"All of these fucking singles… where you going, white boy? Starz?"

He threw the money at his head and rose to his feet.

"Skrappy, help me grab this mothafucka, homie!"

"What...what the fuck are you doing?" Bud's head whipped from left to right between the two men, panicking.

"We already know white men can't jump, but I wanna know if they can fly."

Desmond smiled wickedly, grabbing Bud under his arms. The hoe ass nigga thrashed around as the men carried him over to the window.

"No. Wait... Please. I've gotta painting for—"

"I told you, milk weed... no more paintings."

"Oh, my God, please," Bud pleaded, pissing on himself. The spot at the crotch of his pants grew dark and expanded.

"It's a very special piece I made, especially for him."

"Let him go!" a voice came from the doorway, freezing everyone in their tracks. Premo and Skrappy's heads snapped in the direction that the bone chilling voice came from. A fairly tall Mexican man wearing a duster over a sweatshirt strolled in. His boots echoed on the hardwood floor as he advanced on them. He had short curly hair and an eye-patch over his left eye. The expression on his face said that he was there on business and not bullshit. The aura surrounding him screamed power and sophistication.

"Desmond," Bud's eyes bugged, and he crossed his heart.

"I said, let 'em go', or have you gone deaf?" Desmond's nostrils flared. Premo and Skrappy let go of Bud. He hit the floor on his side, cracking his ribs. He grimaced and howled in pain. Desmond pulled out a lighter and a Cuban cigar. Sticking the overgrown cancer stick into his mouth, he cupped his hand around it and fired it up. He sucked on the end of it three times before he was able to pull smoke into his lungs and then blow it back out into the air. He looked to Bud and said in a thick Spanish accent, "So, where's this painting made especially for me?"

"In the corner…there…" Bud pointed, grimacing.

Desmond looked to something large in the corner that was covered by a white sheet. He gave a nod to Skrappy, and he drew the sheet back. What he saw before him made his face light up with a smile. The painting was of him as Jesus, walking the streets of Mexico and being praised by its people.

"Tito, cover it up. I'll be taking it with me," Desmond told him.

"Does this make us even?" Bud asked, managing a smile through his pain.

"Grab 'em, and hold out his right-hand," Desmond ordered Bullet and Tito. As Bullet and Tito moved in on Bud, he looked around scared and confused.

"Wait a minute! What's this? What's going on?" he asked. He tried to put up a fight, but it was useless. He found himself staring up at Desmond with the hand he used for painting stretched out before him. The look he wore was one of terror as he wondered what the drug lord planned to do to his hand.

Crack!Crack!Crack!Crack!

The bones in Bud's hand crackled and broke as Desmond stomped it with the heel of his boot. Bud's face twisted in agony and tears rolled down his face, splashing on the hardwood floor. Desmond's heel twisted and ground into Bud's hand, and then he stomped it one last time, cracking bones.

Bud sobbed like a little bitch as he bawled on the floor, cradling his broken hand. It was bruised red, blue, and purple, and throbbing something awful. He was sure he'd never use it to make a living again.

"Now we're even," Desmond told him with terrifying eyes. He pulled a tiny zip-lock bag of dope from his suit and tossed it at Bud's side. He snapped his fingers. Right away, Premo and Skrappy picked up the painting and followed him out of the door, leaving their victim whimpering on the floor.

****

Desmond made his way down the long corridor with Premo and Skrappy bringing the painting at his rear. Feeling his cell ring and vibrate inside of his pocket, he pulled it out, and his brows furrowed. This was because he was curious as to why this individual was calling him when he was given specific orders to deal with his cousin.

"Speak," was all he said into the cell phone. As soon as he said this, Pain gave him the rundown on what had happened. Hearing that his relative had been murdered in cold blood caused Desmond's eyes to turn glassy and crevasses to form across his forehead.

"Before we agreed to do business with you guys, I told you that you're responsible for Manny's safety when he crosses over to your side, right?"

Pain took a deep breath and replied, "Right."

His face twisted with hatred.

"I told you that whatever fate he befalls, your entire crew will meet it as well, right?"

Pain blew hot air and ran his hand down his face. He glanced back at Epic and Lil' Joe and shook his head. He then focused his attention back on the conversation that he was having over the telephone.

"Right."

Desmond snatched the cigar out of his mouth and said, "You're dead, nigger… you and your fucking crew of monkeys."

He disconnected the call.

****

Pain shut his eyelids and held the phone to his ear a while longer. He shook his head, hating to hear that him and his niggas had beef with Desmond and his hittas now, but there wasn't shit that he could do, but lock ass with those mothafuckas. There wasn't any way in hell he was going to tuck his tail and run from these old buster ass niggas. Pain dropped the hand that held the phone to his side. Taking a deep breath, he turned around to his home boys and said, "We're at war."

"Fuck, man!" Lil' Joe swung on the air so hard that he dropped his baseball cap.

"Fuck it," Epic said, staring Pain dead in his eyes.

"It's time to get active with these niggas. We at 'em… ASAP."

"That's what it is then… fuck them."

Pain held out his fist. Epic held out his fist and said, "Fuck 'em!"

"Fuck 'em!"

Lil' Joe stuck out his fist too.   One for all, and all for one.

****

Epic had Lil' Joe pull two houses down from the location and murder the headlights of the box Chevy. Epic and Pain pulled their ski masks down over their faces and made sure their bangers were cocked, locked, and ready to spit death.

"Yo, you sure these are the fools, fam?" Pain questioned, tying a black bandana around the lower half of his face. Him, Epic and Lil' Joe were all dressed in all black and rocking beanies.

"Yeah, I'm sure it's them niggas. I told you how my boy hooked it up. I talked to dude and went ova to his spot... fronted like I was gone buy the shit. Nigga had the product that we got taken for the otha night... same red spider stamp and eh thang."

Epic's face balled up, and he locked his jaws, veins bulging out the side of his neck. All that could be seen were his terrifying eyes over the bandana that was over the lower half of his face. He had two nine-millimeter Berettas with silencers on their barrels.

"That's all the fuck I needed to hear. Niggas take our shit and get us twisted with these wild ass wetbacks... nuh unh. On God, we twisting all these may-mays caps back."

Pain finished loading up his forty-five automatic handgun with the silencer on the barrel. His mind was on murder, and his trigger finger was ready to execute those thoughts.

"Fa sho'," Epic nodded and assured him.

"I'ma tighten these fags up, and we gone dip up outta here. You know my motto... murda ain't nothing but a thang."

"Sho' you right."

Pain chambered a bald head copper bullet into his lethal weapon. Epic turned to Lil' Joe.

"Keep a close watch on the house. If anybody comes outta there that ain't us, you soak their asses up, okay?"

"I got chu," the little nigga nodded, a sawed off shotgun in his lap. A thirty-eight bulldog was in the holster on his ankle.

"Good lookin' out."

He dapped him up and then turned to his right-hand man. "Come on, Pain."

Epic and Pain jumped out of the Chevy and shut their doors quietly. Hunched over, they hurried across the street, keeping a close eye on things, guns at their sides. They infiltrated the front yard of the nigga's house that they had hit for all of those bricks. Epic and Pain swept up the front steps. Epic had picked the locks of both the black iron door and the wooden door. He had done this, coming in and out of the house. This made their job of getting inside of the house easy.

Epic quietly opened both of the doors, one by one. He was so careful that the niggas kicking it inside of the living room didn't even hear them coming in. They were all smoking and drinking, watching Pineapple Express on cable TV. Epic and Pain exchanged glances. He gave him orders to take everyone out but to leave the nigga in the stocking cap and Lakers jersey, which was Shorty, alive.

Pain gave his home boy a nod of understanding, and then they handled their business. The two masked up niggas came up, silenced weapons extended and spitting hot fire. Grumbles of agony and blood misted the air. The fools on the couch grimaced, dropping their respective hookas and cups of liquor, splashing it on the floor. Gun smoke wafted in the air, and the killas took a look at all of the chaos that they had created. Everyone in the living room was laid the fuck out, dead, with bleeding black holes in them. The only sound was the loud ass flat screen TV which had splatters of blood on it, running down to the bottom of the television to outline it.

Hearing someone moan in excruciating pain, their heads snapped in the direction from which it came. They looked and saw Shorty holding his stomach, slowly lumbering down the hallway and dripping blood along the way. Pain lifted his forty-five, but Epic signaled to him that he would handle the little man. Taking a knee, he shut one eye and gripped his tool with both gloved hands, curling his finger around the trigger. He waited for the precise moment and squeezed, taking out both of his prey's knees. Shorty collapsed in the hallway, making the sounds of a wounded animal.

"I got this nigga. Check the house for our shit," a scowling Epic ordered, before walking toward the bleeding man, tucking one of his twins in the small of his back. He grabbed the giant by the back of his shirt and pulled him up to his knees, seeing him wincing. Epic looked up and saw that Pain had ducked off inside of the kitchen. He could hear pots and pans clashing as he rummaged underneath the cabinets.

"Where the fuck is our shit, nigga?" Epic hollered in Shorty's wincing face. The little man looked up at him.

"Huh?"

"You ain't tellin' me shit, huh?"

He cracked him upside of his dome with the butt of his Beretta, sending blood sliding down his face. The nigga was dizzy now. He had one eye shut because blood had gotten into it. Epic let his ass crash face first to the floor. He then called out to Pain.

"Yo, check this faggot's bedroom. I'ma get the bathroom. If he lyin', then he dyin'… straight up."

With that said, Pain came down the hallway and slipped inside of the master bedroom, glancing at Shorty as he passed him. Epic went inside of the bathroom, leaving the door open so that he'd have a clear view of the corridor. He kicked over the hamper and spilled all of the dirty clothes. He went through them with his sneaker, hoping to find the bricks.

Coming up empty handed, he rummaged through the bathroom sink. There wasn't shit under there either. He scratched his head, wondering where the fuck the bricks could have been stashed. That's when his eyes landed on the toilet. Using one hand, he took off the toilet's top where you could see the inner workings of it and smiled. Inside were two bricks of cocaine, both stamped with a red spider. He sat both of those shits on the toilet seat's lid and placed the top back on the commode.

"This the nigga that popped me and snatched my chain that night, E."

Pain walked out into the hallway, holding up the gold rope chain with the continent of Africa medallion on it. He wore a shocked expression, but that quickly changed to a more hostile look. His eyebrows arched, and his lips peeled back in a sneer, showcasing his teeth.

"Fuck you get this chain, my nigga?"

He approached Shorty, chain dangling from his hand. Once he was standing over him, he asked him the same question.

"Fuck…fuck y'all niggas, man! You gone kill me, then kill me then!" he hollered out, slowly getting up on his hands, blood dripping from his off of his brow.

"All right, I'ma kill yo' ass then, bitch nigga."

Pain tucked his tool at the small of his back and held his rope chain by both ends, handling it like he was going to use it for strangulation… and he was. Pain quickly looped the chain over Shorty's neck and pulled it back, tightening it against his throat. Shorty's eyes bugged, and his tongue hung out the side of his mouth. He tried to slip his fingers underneath the chain, but his attempts were futile. Before long, his pupils were rolling to the back of his head, and his tongue was hanging further out of his grill. His arms slowly began to grow limp, and they eventually fell at his sides with him gagging above a whisper.

Epic smiled wickedly, watching his home boy get down on the murder.

"You see God yet, nigga? Huh? You see his ass?" Pain gritted, pulling back further on his chain, sweating beneath his ski-mask. His form slightly shook, and he growled. A second later, Shorty went still, and the noise he was making stopped. The thug released him, and he fell on his face, eyes staring up ahead at nothing.

Pain admired his handiwork for a time and then looped his rope chain over his head, tucking it in. He still had his respect in the streets for putting it down on niggas that had violated him after he'd gotten his chain stolen, but once they saw him rocking his old shit, they'd know he wasn't letting shit slide no matter how old the beef was. Pulling his ski-mask up, Pain wiped the sweat from his forehead with the back of his fist, before pulling it down over his face.

"You got all the bricks?" he asked that nigga, Epic.

"Nah, just two of them shits were here… fuckin' midget must've sold the rest of 'em."

He dropped the blocks inside of a pillow he'd taken from the master bedroom and slung it over his shoulder, meeting up with his right-hand at the center of the hallway.

"Fuck!" Pain cursed. Pissed off, he stomped Shorty's face until it looked like bloody hamburger meat, specks of blood on the leg of his jeans.

"Come on. Let's go."

Epic nudged him as he crossed his path heading down the hallway. Pain took one last look at Shorty before following his home boy out of the house.

CHAPTER ELEVEN

Treasure stood out in front of Blessyn's condo, waiting on the Uber that she'd ordered. Every so often, she found herself glancing down at her watch. She'd ordered the car fifteen minutes ago, and he was supposed to have been there three minutes ago. She called him twice, and he promised that he was on his way. He gave her some excuse about catching a flat tire and having to change it, but she wasn't sure if she believed him or not. All she knew was she was ready to go home and have herself a drink to unwind. Hearing her cell phone ring, Treasure looked at the name on the screen and then answered it.

"What's up? Hold on."

Using her shoulder, Treasure held the cellular to her ear while she fished through her bag. Coming up with an ink pen and an old receipt, she pressed both of them against her thigh. As she listened to what she was being told, she jotted it down with her pen.

"Alright, I got it. I perform at The Staple Center Thursday at 4:00 for the NBA championship game. Okay, gimme the info to the hotel I'ma be staying at."

She jotted down the rest of the information and looked at the receipt, still holding the cell phone to her ear.

"Yeah, I got it. Thanks, boo… smooches."

She kissed her booking agent through the phone and disconnected the call. Afterwards, she scrolled through her old text messages between herself and Pain. As she read through the messages, she felt a stinging in her eyes. From this, she knew that tears weren't far behind. She couldn't help it though. The texts reminded her of how much in love they were back then. Treasure had been Pain's ride or die. She had him at his best and his worse… when he was teetering between life and death…

Boom!

The double doors of the emergency ward flew open. The hospital staff rushed Pain along on a gurney, tearing open his shirt and exposing the black bleeding holes in him. His eyes were hooded, and his pupils moved around lazily. He tried to say something and winded up coughing up blood.

"Hold on, baby, Hold on!" a crying Treasure told him, running alongside the gurney, clutching his crimson stained hand. The blood on it was drying. Her face was drenched, and she couldn't stop the tears from falling. It looked like she had been splashed in the face with a bucket of water. She pulled the black bandana free from around his forehead and kissed him sweetly there.

"Ma'am, I'm going to need you to let 'em go. We've got it from here," one of the doctors told her. She wasn't paying him any attention though. Her main focus was on the man whose life she had saved earlier that night.

Tears danced at the corners of Pain's eyes, and he was staring up at the ceiling smiling. Treasure frowned, because it seemed as if he was looking at someone or something. She looked where his line of vision ended and didn't find anything. Then, that's when it came to her that he was probably looking up at an angel or a deceased loved one.

"No, no, no, stay with me, Trip! Stay with me!" she begged, tears bursting out of her eyes. Pain's eyes stayed glued to the ceiling as he was being rushed down the hallway.

"Miss, you've gotta go. Let us do our job," the doctor that had spoken to her earlier said, pulling her hand free from the

patient. Slowly, her palm and fingers released his hand. Pain appeared as if he was trying to say something when one of the hospital staff looped an oxygen mask over his nose and mouth. Inside of the mask fogged with each weak breath that he took, lungs inflating and deflating.

Standing where she was inside of the corridor, Treasure cupped her hands around her mouth and called out to Pain.

"Keep fighting, Trip! Keep fighting, baby!"

Her words echoed throughout the hallway as she stood where she was, watching the hospital staff rush Pain to emergency surgery. She wiped the wetness from her face and sniffled, still looking on. The gurney and the staff grew smaller and smaller until they disappeared. Treasure lingered there for a moment, looking at Pain's bandana before eventually walking off to the women's restroom.

****

Treasure stood in the women's restroom mirror, peeling off her blood stained leather jacket and blouse. She turned her head from left to right, taking in her appearance. She had splotches of blood on her face, neck, and chest... even her hands. Hell, she even had the shit in her hair. All of it had dried on her. Treasure had never experienced anything like she had that night, and she was sure she'd probably never go through anything again that would top it. That she was sure of... at least she hoped. Hurrying over to the paper towel dispenser, she pulled a few of them loose and used it to blow her nose. Once she was done, she balled the paper towel up and tossed it into the trash can. Placing her hands on the edge of the sink, she took a few deep breaths and shut her eyelids briefly. When she peeled them back open, she had calmed herself a little and moved to handle her business.

Dispensing the pink foam into her palm, Treasure began washing herself up. She washed every inch of her body that had blood on it. Looking down while she was taking care of the task at hand, she saw pink water swirling down the drain. The blood had mixed in with the water and dyed it that color. Treasure pumped some more of the pink foam soap into her palm and lathered her hair until it was completely white. She leaned over into the sink, where the faucet was still running, and rinsed her hair out. Afterwards, she squeezed her hair out and whipped it back, smacking herself at the middle of her back. It was long and curly now, having been washed.

Treasure wiped off her jacket and washed her blouse under the flowing water with soap. She slipped on the blouse and then the leather jacket, adjusting it to her liking. The faucet was still running this entire time. Next, she looked to Pain's bandana. It was lying on the neighboring sink where she'd left it when she first entered the restroom. She picked it up and stared at it, marveling it. Once she turned to her reflection in the mirror, she tied the bandana around her forehead like its owner had. She promised herself that if Pain died that night that she'd wear it for as long as she lived, but she was honestly hoping that she didn't have to.

As soon as Treasure turned the water off, her cellular started ringing, and she looked at it. Daddy was on the screen. A relieved expression crossed her face. She'd called her father on her way to the hospital, and he promised her that he'd be there as soon as he could. Treasure pushed open the women's restroom door. Out in the hallway, she found her father and his niggas chopping it up. Her old man was on his cellular, attempting to call her again. Suddenly, her cell rang inside of her bag when she pulled it out. It was her father. Grief was on *the screen. Still looking down at the cellular, she pushed opened the restroom's door and crossed the threshold.*

****

Buddah tapped Grief and pointed Treasure out to him. Seeing his baby girl, the OG disconnected the call and stashed his cell. Hurriedly, he walked in her direction, taking in his surroundings. As soon as he reached his daughter, he led her back inside of the restroom by pressing his hand against the lower half of her back. He locked the door behind them and turned to her, walking over to the sinks. Cupping his daughter's face in his hands, he looked into her eyes and asked if she was okay. She nodded yes, and he hugged her affectionately, kissing her on the cheek.

"What exactly happened out there?" Grief asked curiously. Treasure gave her old man the rundown for the first time. She told him everything that she couldn't over the jack. He was a street nigga, and he schooled her to the game early in life. She knew the lifestyle inside and out, not to mention, she abided by the rules. Little mama was truly daddy's little girl.

"Okay... alright," he said, turning on the faucet water. Next, he pulled a black jar with a dirty green lid from out of his overcoat's pocket and a toothbrush. He had her rub the greasy substance in the jar on her hands and then he scrubbed under her fingernails. Afterwards, she washed her hands clean. This was so there wouldn't be any traces of gunpowder residue on her hands. Anytime a gunshot victim entered the emergency ward, the police were called to come asking questions. The OG wanted to make sure that his daughter had all bases covered when they came around. He sure as hell didn't want her catching a charge behind busting that gun. No

one knew as good as him how hard she was working to get into the music industry.

"Listen, when them folks come, you tell 'em you didn't see what happened. You fell asleep in Trip's car and woke up to gunfire. You got it?"

She nodded yes.

"Good. Now... did you clean yo' prints off that burner and toss it in the gutta like I told you to?"

"Yes, daddy."

"Good, girl."

He gripped her shoulders and kissed her on the forehead.

"Come on."

He took her by the hand and lead her toward the door, pushing it open. As soon as they crossed the threshold, they found Skylar. Her eyes had swollen so much that she looked like she had a fight with someone. Standing on either side of her was Epic and Lil' Joe. Both of their faces were fixed with hostile expressions.

"Treasure."

Skylar spotted her friend and ran toward her with her arms open. Treasure went running toward her too. They met at the halfway mark and hugged like sisters do during a family tragedy. The best friends rocked from side to side, crying their eyes out. Skylar broke their embrace, holding her at arm's length.

"Give it to me straight, sis."

She wiped her tearing eyes with her curled finger.

"Did...did they hit bro bro up bad? Does it look like he will be okay?"

Treasure hung her head and shook it. Skylar broke down sobbing, wailing at the top of her lungs and drawing the attention of some the hospital staff.

"What the fuck y'all lookin' at, huh?" Epic addressed them all, taking in all of their faces.

"Can't y'all see my family is going through a hard time right now? Huh? I suggest you mothafuckas keep y'all selves busy like ain't none of this shit happenin', 'fore I whip one of you niggas or one of you bitches out cha shoes or some shit."

His ranting got the staff back to doing what the fuck they were paid for, acting like Pain's loved ones weren't even there.

Skylar finally calmed herself down and addressed her sister from another mister.

"Okay... alright."

She took deep breaths, licked her lips, and started up again.

"How many times was Trip shot? Was he hit in the arm, chest, or head? Where? And please, please, please, tell me the truth," *she begged Treasure, holding her hand in both of hers. Treasure shut her eyelids briefly and took a deep breath, slumping her shoulders. She peeled her eyelids opened and spoke.*

"He got shot like eleven times..."

Skylar gasped and fresh tears misted in her eyes as she held her hands to the lower half of her face.

"As far as him making it..." *she shut her eyelids and bit down on her bottom lip, nostrils flaring. Tears came bursting out of her eyes as she tried to find the strength to finish telling her home girl what she needed to hear.*

"Treasure, just tell me... please."

Skylar jumped up and down anxiously, hands together. She shook her head and looked up at her, staring her right in the eyes.

"I don't...I don't think he's gonna make it."

"Oooooh God, whyyyyyy?"

She looked up at the ceiling, holding up her clenched fists. Her entire form quivered and veins bulged in her neck and forehead. Her mouth was wide open as she hollered. Saliva webbed inside of her mouth.

"Haven't my brotha and I been through enough? Huh?"

Fat Rat, Buddah, Grief, Epic, and Lil' Joe all hung their heads. They all knew how hard Trip and Skylar had it growing up. You would have thought that the powers that be would have saw fit to give the poor kids a break, but in this case, they obviously didn't. It was hardship after hardship with them. They rarely got a chance to breathe, and when they did, they just knew a rough time wasn't too far behind.

Skylar collapsed in Lil' Joe's arms, sobbing her heart out as he did his best to console her.

"Baby girl," Grief nudged his daughter and nodded toward the emergency entrance. When she looked, she found two pink faced detectives in cheap ass suits, shields on their belts. Their blue eyes scanned the room, stopping once they landed on Treasure. Having sighted her, they started in her direction. While they were in route, Grief kept his eyes on them and whispered into his daughter's ear to remember what he told her what to say. She nodded.

"Are you Treasure Jones?" the detective with the balding scalp asked. When she nodded yes, he introduced himself as Detective Reynolds and his partner as Detective Panella.

"We'd like to interview you about the shooting that occurred tonight involving you and your boyfriend. You want to come with us?"

"Sure."

"Right this way."

Placing his hand at her lower back, he led her out into the hallway. It was there that the detectives went through a couple of rounds of questions, trying to slip her up. None of that shit worked though. Treasure had been taught well by her father. The OG was seasoned. There wasn't an aspect of the game that he hadn't went through, so obviously, little mama got through those questions with ease. When it was done, she was left with a card that one of the detectives had given her. Once the detectives had disappeared through the double doors of the emergency room, Treasure ripped the card into pieces. She turned her back and headed back to where her people were, leaving the torn up pieces of card falling like snowflakes from out of the air.

"How'd it go?" Grief asked his daughter, hand on her shoulder.

"How you told me it would."

He cracked a smile and said, "Good, girl."

"Are you the family of Trip Turner?" a tall Indian doctor in glasses and scrubs addressed Skylar.

"Yes, I'm his sister, and everyone else here are his uncles, cousins and brothers," she responded. Everyone assembled behind Skylar, waiting to see what the good doctor had to say in regards of their loved one. He gave them the rundown in words someone in his field may have understood better. What he had relayed left everyone glancing at one another and scratching their heads.

"In other words?" Skylar inquired, a line creasing her forehead. He took a deep breath and removed his glasses, massaging the bridge of his nose. Once he slipped the glasses back on, he went on to tell her exactly what he meant.

"I'm afraid your brother may not talk or walk again..."

"Jesus."

Skylar's eyes rolled back in her head, and she collapsed in Treasure's arms. Treasure lay on the floor with Skylar in her arms, smacking her face and trying to get her to come to. Her eyelids were shut, and her head nudged to the left as it was smacked. The rest of the men were surrounding her while her father was talking to the doctor, trying to get some more information on Pain's condition. The bad news got Epic and Lil' Joe all fired up. They paced the floor, talking shit and swearing revenge for their home boy.

"I don't give a fuck, niggas gettin' smashed for hittin' the homie!" Epic went off.

"That's on me! These faggots gone feel it behind mine! That's on everything!" Lil' Joe popped off at the mouth. His words echoed throughout the hospital, coming down the hallways.

****

The night had wound down, and everyone was allowed to see Pain, thanks to Skylar showing her natural black ass. Treasure opted to see him last because she wanted to spend time with him alone. She didn't want anyone intruding on the time she had with him. Grief and his niggas waited in the lobby for her while she went to go see Pain.

When Treasure entered the young man's room, she had to grab a hold of the wall to stay upon her wobbling legs. Wetness accumulated at the corners of her eyes, but she wiped it away with her thumbs. The young man she'd been out on a date with just hours ago appeared to be hanging on by a thread. He was laid up in a cast iron bed, ashy and clad in a pair of boxer briefs that had splotches of blood on them. He was hooked up to all kinds of machinery to keep him alive and breathing. The noise the medical equipment made was the only sounds inside of his dimly lit room. Homie was teetering between life and death, but the expression on his face was solemn. His torso, arms, and legs were wrapped in bandages that were caked with blood.

Treasure approached his bedside, pulling a chair along with her. She took it and planted it beside his bed and sat down, taking his hand into hers.

"Hey, Trip," she started off, caressing his hand.

"The night was pretty wild for our second date, huh?"

All that could be heard were the sounds of the medical machinery and the chattering outside the door by the staff as she shut her eyelids briefly and tried to gather herself. She could feel herself about to fall apart, but she wanted to stay strong, if not for herself, then for him.

"Man, I never would have thought shit would have popped off the way it did. I mean, one minute, we were chilling in the car and listening to music, then the next, some nigga comes outta nowhere firing."

Flashes of the shooter blasting on Pain and him running for cover went through her mind. She could hear the gunshots so loud and clear that it felt like she was right there.

"Anyway," Treasure shook her thoughts of the shooting from her mental.

"I don't wanna talk about that any more. I'd much rather spend this time talking about you. I had a great time tonight at the Santa Monica Pier. It's been a while since I had some fun like that."

A smile stretched across her beautiful face as she caressed Pain's hand with her own.

"I would have never thought in a million years that I'd find myself falling for you like this. I mean, I always found you attractive, but I just thought things would always remain the way that they have between us."

She took the time to swallow her spit before continuing.

"Anyway, we entered this thing of ours knowing that things could go south, and we may not even end up feeling one another like that, but that turned out not even being the case, because we got it bad for one another. Mannnnn, who would have thought?"

She stopped, her forehead crinkling, seeing his long fingernails.

"Damn, boo. Lemme clip these nails for you. You're looking like mothafucking Teen Wolf by the hand."

She fished inside of her bag until she found the fingernail clippers. She rested his hand in her lap and went about handling the task at hand. As she was clipping his nails, she glanced back at his toes, his nails there needed to be cut too.

"I'ma hook up them feet too. Fuck it, my nigga, I'ma hook you up with a pedi and a mani, 'cause you sho' 'nough need it. Whatever bitch you were fucking with before me didn't believe in taking her nigga to a nail shop. That's for damn sure."

Treasure went on talking to Pain like he could respond, being that he was in a coma. From what she'd heard, people that were in a coma could hear their loved ones talking to them, although they weren't awake. Anyway, Treasure did Pain's hands and feet. She even gave him a sponge bath.

Afterwards, she pulled out her iPod and let him listen to the song that they were listening to inside of his car on the night he was shot. The song was one that she had recorded just days prior in the studio. It was going to be placed on her demo to send out to studios and for her to hustle to any heads that were looking for something new to groove to.

Treasure let Pain listen to three songs before she turned off the iPod. She kissed him tenderly on his lips and walked to the door. Stopping in the doorway, she looked back over her shoulder at Pain.

"Stay strong, baby boy. You got this. See you tomorrow."

She kissed her palm and blew him a kiss. She then turned out the lights and made her departure.

Over the next three weeks, Treasure visited Pain at the hospital. She brought him flowers and cards and let him listen to the music that she'd been recording on her iPod. Although there was never any reaction from him hearing the music, she still played it for him. She'd continued to talk to him too, imagining what he'd say back to her.

Treasure pulled her iPod out of her bag and placed the earbuds inside of Pain's ears. Her thumb went through the device until she found the track that she had recorded last night. Once she came upon it, she pressed play and stuck it into his partially opened hand. She cranked the volume on the iPod and looked up at Pain, watching for any reaction to the song. Treasure ran two of her acrylic nails up and down his tattooed arm soothingly. Observing Pain's facial features as the music played in his ears...

This willpower, this spirit, it's too solid
They can't break it
I won't stop I can't stop, I'm built for this. I'ma make it

*I will live, I will talk, I will walk. I'm dedicated
I will live, I will talk, I will walk. I'm dedicated.
I'm unstttttopppablllllle, they say I won't but I'ma talk agaiiiin
I'm unstttttopppablllllle, they say I won't but I'ma walk agaiiiin
I'm unstttttopppablllllle, I'ma do it alllllllllll agaiiiin
I'm unstttttopppablllllle, there's no way that I cannot wiiiiiiiiiiin*

Seeing a flicker of movement at the corner of her eye, Treasure looked but didn't see anything. She focused her attention back on the object of her affection, still running her nails up and down his arm. She saw the flicker of movement again out the corner of her eye, but this time, she didn't turn around. Nah, she waited a moment, and then, her head snapped in that direction. Tears welled up in her eyes and her lips quivered, as she smacked her hands over her mouth. Looking to his face, she saw his eyelids twitching. When she looked down, she saw his toes twitching. The music continued to play in his earbuds.

*I'm unstttttopppablllllle, they say I won't but I'ma talk agaiiiin
I'm unstttttopppablllllle, they say I won't but I'ma walk agaiiiin
I'm unstttttopppablllllle, I'ma do it alllllllllll agaiiiin
I'm unstttttopppablllllle, there's no way that I cannot wiiiiiiiiiiin*

"Oh my God, he's moving! He's moving!"

Treasure shot to her feet and ran out of the room, her sneakers screeching on the floor. She ran down the hallway, garnering every one's attention that she came across. Her reflection shown on the waxed floor as she flew down the corridor, her heels coming close to hitting her in her ass. Treasure came across the doctor that was taking care of Pain.

"Haa! Haa! Haa! Haa! Dr. Stanford! Dr. Stanford!" she stopped before a short copper skinned doctor with a balding scalp and thick lens glasses. Huffing and puffing out of breath, Treasure held the doctor at arm's length.

"Haa! Haa! Haa! Haa! He's alive! He's alive! Haa! Haa! Haa!" she panted, out of breath, and swallowed the spit in her throat.

"Calm down! Calm down!" he told her, holding her at arm's length also. Once she seemed to be under control, he continued.

"Now, what did you see exactly?"

Treasure reported to him exactly what she saw. He took the stethoscope from around his neck, and they went charging down the corridor together.

CHAPTER TWELVE

Three weeks later

Lil' Joe pushed Pain in a wheelchair as he and Epic strolled the hospital grounds. The two of them seemed to be engrossed in conversation, oblivious to Treasure and Skylar watching them through the window of the cafeteria. Leaves fell from the trees that Lil' Joe, Epic, and Pain were moving beneath. They went from left to right on their way to the ground where they made crunching sounds as they were rolled over by the wheelchair.

"You didn't see the nigga's face or anything we could go on to find 'em?" Epic asked seriously. He wore a durag and a hoodie that made the outlining of his Kevlar vest slightly visible.

"Nah," Pain shook his head. "My nigga was masked up. Every part of him was covered up. All I know is that he was short and black. I knew he was a brotha, 'cause I could see his complexion through the holes of his ski-mask."

"Damn," he slammed his fist into his palm as he walked. "You got my word, Pain. We gone find this mothafucka that turned his gun on you."

Pain nodded his understanding.

"Straight up. You good as blood, family. This nigga popping you is the same as him taking a shot at one of us."

Epic nodded in agreement.

"The streets gone feel this one. That's on everything."

"No doubt," Epic cosigned. At that moment, his cell rang, and he glanced at the screen. Seeing who it was, he answered it and told the caller to hold on. Pressing his cell to his chest, he turned to Pain.

"Yo', bruh bruh, I gotta take this, but I'ma check you later and see how you doing... yah mean?"

When Pain nodded his understanding, he hugged him and kissed him on the cheek.

"We gone get chu yo' chain back too. Don't even sweat it."

Lil' Joe slapped hands with him and placed his hand on top of his, staring him directly in the eyes.

"We gone get this nigga, big bruh. That's my word."

Pain gave Lil' Joe a nod and watched him and Epic's backs as they walked off. Epic was talking on his cell, and Lil' Joe was running up behind him, pulling his sagging pants up on his ass. Hearing footsteps behind him, Pain swung around in his wheelchair. At his rear, he discovered Treasure, Skylar, Grief, and his niggas. Grief adjusted his apple-jack and fixed the collar of his overcoat before stepping to the young thug. Everyone else stood behind him like they were his entourage. They watched as he kneeled down before Pain and looked up into his eyes.

"I'm 'bout to get up outta here. I got some business to take care of, but listen... I'ma keep my ear to the streets. If I get any info on the bastard that put chu in a bad way...well, you know how gangstas get down."

"Sho' 'nough." Pain replied. With that having been said, the OG shook his hand and patted it with the other. Looking him dead in his eyes, he gave him a nod that assured him that his shooter would be brought to street justice. Afterwards, he kissed his daughter on the cheek and motioned for his niggas to follow him, making his way toward the elevators so he could get down to the parking lot complex.

Pain turned around to Skylar. From the look on her face, he could tell that she'd been crying for most of his hospitalization. Her eyes were still quite puffy, and her nose was red. She looked like she had the flu or some shit.

"You finna get on outta here too, bird?" Pain questioned.

"Yeah, I gotta go to work, but Tank is 'posed to pick me up, so we gone swing by in the A.M," she assured him.

"You ain't gotta do that. A nigga up. I'm good now."

"So what. We damn near lost yo' ass, Trip. You aren't 'posed to be alive. Truthfully, I gotta make sure this shit isn't a dream, so me and my boo thang are rolling by here to check on you tomorrow morning. I won't take no for an answer, so hush now."

She leaned closer and embraced him, tightening her arms around him. Her body rocked, and tears trickled down her cheeks, causing her to sniffle.

"I love you, bro bro." she told him as he rubbed his hand up and down her back. It felt good to hug his sister again. It was moments like this that reminded him all over again how much he loved her. Pain and Skylar never knew their parents. They'd given them to the system when they were just babies. The siblings grew up in foster care, until they eventually escaped and made the streets their home. Together, they stole, robbed, scammed, and petty hustled to keep their heads above water. Their hard times strengthened their bond, guaranteeing nothing or no one would ever come between them…short of death.

"I love you too, sis."

He kissed her on the side of her face, and she kissed him back. Skylar broke their embrace and wiped the tears from her dripping eyes. She then turned to Treasure and hugged her.

"I love you too, girl. Take care of my brotha now. That's my heart."

"I got chu faded, boo."

Treasure kissed her on the cheek. Skylar adjusted her purse's strap on her shoulder as she sauntered past her brother. She patted him on his shoulder and kept on toward the elevator. Treasure and Pain watched her walk away for a time before focusing on one another.

"Hey, gorgeous," he greeted her with a smile.

"Hey, handsome," she smiled back.

"You wanna take a ride with me?"

She looked to him sitting in the wheelchair and remembered he'd been shot eleven times. Her forehead deepened with lines, and she looked back up at him.

"I don't know, Trip. I don't wanna hurt you. I mean, you've been shot and—"

"Don't sweat it," he told her.

"I took a couple of pain killas, so I'm straight. Climb yo' pretty ass up on my ride."

He spun around in circles in his wheelchair. Then, keeping the wheels up, he rocked the chair backwards and forwards.

"You sure?" she angled her head.

"Positive."

"Okay."

She cautiously sat down on his lap.

"Arghhhhh!" he threw his head back hollering at the top of his lungs, eyelids stretched wide open. A frightened Treasure jumped up out of his lap, checking to see if he was okay. Her hands gently touched his body as if he was so fragile that he'd break.

"Oh my God! Are you all right?" she panicked.

"Oooooh yeah, hahahahahahahaha!" he gave a toothy laugh and slapped his knee.

"You asshole!" she playfully punched him in his arm, causing him to ball up but continue to laugh.

"Got that ass good. Now come on, and sit on big daddy's lap." He patted his lap.

"All right now, but don't play."

"I won't."

"I'm serious now."

She raised an eyebrow and pointed at him.

"Okay. Damn."

Treasure eased herself onto his lap. Once she'd gotten good and settled, she sighed with relief.

"And away we go," he started off, rolling the wheelchair.

"You know, I wanted to thank you for saving my life that night. If it wasn't for you, the homies would have been rocking rest in peace T-shirts and pouring out forties, nah mean?"

"You were in trouble. I had to do something," she told him.

"I couldn't just standby while he smoked you."

"Still... thanks."

"No problem. That's what will happen if anybody tries running up on my man again...shit!" Treasure's eyelids snapped open, realizing that she'd referred to him as her man. She couldn't help it though. She was feeling him from the beginning. The chemistry was there, so it rolled off of her tongue so naturally.

"What? Yo' man?"

His lips stretched across his face and curled at their ends, creating a smile. Embarrassed, she smacked both of her hands over her mouth.

"I'm sorry. I didn't mean it like—"

Before she could finish, he was taking her by the face and shoving his tongue inside of her mouth, angling his head as he kissed her. When he pulled back from her mouth, he was smiling, and she was looking like she was drunk off of his kiss. His thumb caressed her cheek as he sat there, staring into her eyes.

"You said it right. I'm your man, and you're my woman," he told her.

"From this day forward, you're mine. I bet not catch yo' lil' ass giving no otha nigga no play, or I'ma slump that ass... real shit."

"I bet not catch yo' big ass giving none of these hoes out here no play, or I'll knock you, and her ass the fuck out... real shit."

She wore a mesmerized expression on her face, held captive by the thought of being his woman. It was without a doubt in her mind that she always wanted to be his and always would be his...forever.

"Long as we understand one another, lil' mama."

He started back rolling the wheelchair.

"You wanna know something?"

"Sure? What's up?"

Curiosity enveloped her face.

"I died on that operation table," he admitted to her as he rolled the wheelchair. Treasure frowned. This was her first time hearing this since he'd awaken from a coma.

"Really? Did you make it to heaven or hell?"

He stared her in her eyes for a second then looked ahead again, moving the chair along the path.
"Hell."
She gasped and looked at him like she couldn't believe him.
"How do you know? I mean, did you see—"
"Yeah. I saw him... and the fire and brimstone."
He kept it one hundred.
"I made a deal with him, too. I sold my soul."
She grabbed him by his bottom jaw and looked him in his eyes.
"Nuh unh, don't play me. For real, for real?"
"Straight up," he assured her.
"What chu sell yo' soul for?"
"I told The Prince of Darkness that if he allowed me a lil' more time here on earth with you, then he could have my soul... no strings attached... and here I am."
"Nuh unh," she shook her head in disbelief.
"I don't believe you."
When she said this, he stopped the wheelchair and looked her in her face, never blinking. He raised his hand up, palm showing.
"My right hand to God, I sold my soul to the Devil so that I could come back to you."
She searched his eyes to see if he was sincere. As far as she could see, he was being completely honest.
"You came back for me?" her forehead crinkled.
"Yes," he nodded truthfully. Cupping his face, she brought him in closer to her face and they kissed hard and emotionally. Afterwards, she laid her head against his chest and her hand against his waistline. She stared up at him and

smiled. He smiled back and got back to rolling the wheelchair. He took the elevator to the roof of the hospital where he could overlook his city. It was here that he and his lady watched the sunset. By the time the sun was halfway gone, the skyline was yellow and burnt orange. Looking down, Pain saw that Treasure had fallen asleep. He kissed her on top of the head and laid his head against hers, shutting his eyelids for some much needed rest.

Treasure rode in the backseat with tears streaming down her cheeks, mascara running. She sniffled and wiped her nose with the back of her fist. Seeing the driver of the Uber glance up at her through the rearview mirror, she searched through her bag until she found what she was looking for. Pulling out a small round compact mirror, which she flipped open with her thumb, she looked at her reflection. She looked a fucking mess. Sniffling, she looked inside of her bag for some tissue, but she couldn't find any.

"Here ya go, miss."

The driver slammed the glove box shut and handed her a couple of napkins over his shoulder. She thanked him and dried her cheeks. Once she was done, she went on to fix her makeup. Afterwards, she placed the mirror back inside of the bag and focused her attention out of the back window, watching the scenery. Once she made it back home, she thanked the driver and left him with a fifty-dollar tip. She made her way up the steps of her baby mansion and let herself in, arming the alarm system once she'd gotten inside. Heading inside of the kitchen, she fixed herself a glass of something that would have her feeling real nice. Bracing herself up against the counter, she took casual sips from the glass. Fresh tears manifested in her eyes. After sitting the glass down on the island, she looked up to the ceiling with her hands together in prayer.

Treasure shut her eyelids and said, "Please, God, grant me the strength that I need to stop loving this nigga so that I can move on. I don't want to hurt no more."

Tears jetted down her cheeks, and she wiped it away with the back of her hand. She squeezed her eyelids tight as she guzzled down the last of the alcohol and sat the glass down on the island. Walking toward the living room, she peeled off her clothing until she was in her bra and panties. Her clothes were left in piles in her wake. Stopping at the fireplace, she got a nice fire going and plopped down upon the couch. Lying down, she buried her face in the crease of her forearm and cried her eyes out.

CHAPTER THIRTEEN

Epic pulled up in front of Lil' Joe's house and threw the Chevy into park. He took the blunt that he was smoking before they went to Pain's house from between his lips and blew out a cloud of smoke. He then turned to Lil' Joe. That mothafucka was laid back in the seat, looking half dead and shit.

"We at cho spot, home boy," Epic told him and then took another pull from his blunt. When Lil' Joe didn't respond, he called his name several more times, but he still didn't reply. After this, Epic tapped his bleezy above the ashtray, dumping grayish black ashes. Once he had done this, the head of it was glowing ember, smoke wafting from it. Smiling fiendishly once again, he pressed the ember into Lil' Joe's cheek. When ember met flesh, it sizzled, and he winced, smacking his hand over his wound. His head snapped in Epic's direction, and he looked at him like he was crazy.

"Fuck you do that for, man?" Lil' Joe's eyebrows arched, and his nose scrunched up. He was pissed off, but when he saw that nine-millimeter lying in his lap, he humbled himself. Epic saw the change in his little homie's mood and chuckled a little.

"Relax... I called yo' lil' punk ass like a hunnit times. You didn't respond, so I did what I had to do to wake yo' ass up. You home, nigga."

Staring out of Lil' Joe's window, he nodded to his house. Lil' Joe's head whipped around to his window, and he looked like he was surprised to see his house. He felt a little better seeing that he was home. This was because he was trying to get the fuck away from Epic's crazy ass.

"Alright... I'm outta here, folks."

Lil' Joe slapped hands with Epic and hopped out of the Chevy, slamming the door shut behind him. Epic watched him jog across the lawn of his house and then suddenly stop. Seeing this, he smiled again like there was something that only he knew. Looking everywhere but in the little nigga's direction, he counted down from five, and just like he thought, Lil' Joe had come back to his ride. Lil' Joe ducked down inside of the window and locked eyes with him, licking his lips.

"Yo, uh... you got any more of that shit left from earlier?"

"What shit?" Epic frowned like he didn't know what the fuck he was talking about, but in actuality, he did. He just wanted to hear his little punk ass ask for it.

"You know, the..." he pretended to be lighting up a stem of crack.

"My nigga, what the fuck do you want? Be specific about the shit 'cause you really startin' to piss me the fuck off!"

Epic faked like he was mad, but he was really playing that nigga. He really wanted him to tell him that he wanted the crack that he was blazing up earlier. Lil' Joe looked away and took a deep breath. He really didn't want to ask for it straight out, but he was trying to experience that same high that he had earlier that night. Running his hands down his face and taking yet another deep breath, he looked back to a very unhappy Epic.

"I want that bundle of crack that you gave me to get right earlier tonight."

Epic's lips stretched across his face and created a broad smile.

"Now, was that that hard, homie?"

Without waiting for him to reply, he popped open the glove box and pulled out the bundle. As soon as Lil' Joe saw it, his eyes got big, and he smiled, licking his lips. He went to grab the bundle, and that nigga, Epic, snatched it back, still smiling.

"Tell me, what chu 'bout to do with this shit?" he asked, wearing a jovial expression.

"You know what I'ma do with it, my nigga."

"No, I don't. For all I know, you probably finna sling it to a fiend."

Lil' Joe found himself getting frustrated and annoyed. He didn't know why Epic's ass was giving him such a hard time. All he wanted to do was get high, and this cock sucka was prolonging it.

"I'm not slinging nothing. I'ma blaze that shit up soon as I hit the door."

Epic held the bundle out, and Lil' Joe snatched it, running back to the house like he couldn't wait to get inside and smoke it. Laughing manically, Epic cranked up his ride and dipped off down the street.

****

After the murders were carried out, Pain found himself lying in bed with his hands clasped behind his head. He was bare chested and staring up at the ceiling. The light inside of his bedroom was out, but the illumination from the light post on the curb shone on the upper half of his body. As of now, the murders that occurred earlier that night were already at the back of his mind. He had been there and done that before. Nah, his thoughts were on Treasure… the woman that blew into his life and stole his heart. Since their first date, he knew that she was the one he wanted to give his last name to. Once he started fucking with her, he started thinking about marriage, kids, 401Ks and family vacations… shit that he never thought when it came to other females. His thug ass had always been about fucking chicks and counting grips, but the moment he started entertaining Treasure, all of that changed.

Pain shut his eyelids, and a smirk formed on his lips as he thought back to a happier time between him and Treasure…

A smiling Treasure lay with the side of her face pressed against Pain, playing with his chest hair. Her hair was wild, and she was shiny from perspiration. They both were, for that matter. A grinning Pain stared down at the top of his lady's head, running his strong hand up and down her back while the other was buried into the flesh of her thick thigh. She suddenly looked up at him smiling. He smiled too. It was then that they kissed, and she caressed the side of his face.

"I love you," she told him, staring deeply into his brown eyes. It was like he could feel her looking inside of him and into his soul.

"I love you too."

He held her gaze. He never broke it as he wrapped his arms around her, the warmth of his embrace heating up her body as well as making her feel safe. Stopping their kissing, she laid up against him and shut her eyelids. He shut his eyelids as well, embracing her just a little more. Right when they'd gotten comfortable, her cell rang. She stayed put, snuggling up closer to him, but his eyelids peeled open. He went to answer it, but she stopped him.

"Nuh unh... you promised that it's just me and you this weekend."

She held tight to his wrist as the cell phone continued to ring.

"Umm... excuse me, sweetheart, but that's not my phone that's ringing... that's yours."

Treasure's forehead wrinkled as she wondered who it was, because she told everyone not to call her since she and her boo were spending the weekend together. A look came over her face like she'd finally realized something and she crawled over him. Her titties dangled as she reached over him and grabbed her cell. Looking at the screen, she saw that it was a

212 area code. This was a New York area code and that's where that mothafucka that owned Big Willie records was from. Treasure damn near broke her neck answering the device. She hurriedly placed it to his ear and listened closely, pacing the room naked. Pain sat up on his elbows and looked over at his girl.

"Babe, who is that?" *he asked her curiously.*

"Shhhhh," *she hushed him with a finger to her lips. Continuing to pace the floor, she listened closely to what she was being told to her, and a smile grew broader and broader across her face.*

"Okay, okay. Thank you, thank you, thank you."

She disconnected the call and jumped around excitedly.

"What? What's the good news?" *he smiled, seeing his lady so amped up. She jumped on him and threw her arms around his neck, kissing him all over his face. He shut his eyelids, laughing and chuckling.*

"Are you gonna tell me what's up?"

Treasure sat up on her knees in bed.

"Okay."

She took a deep breath, rubbing her hands together. She smiled and licked her lips, barely able to contain her joy.

"Guess who's signing to Big Willie records?" *she smiled hard and clapped her hands rapidly. Pain's eyelids snapped* open, and he hollered. Grabbing her under her arms, he spun around and around with her. They chuckled and smiled.

"Congratulations, baby. You did it! You fucking did it."

He cheered, spinning her around and around. The scenery around them looked like flashes as they rotated. Pain sat Treasure down breathing hard, chest inflating and deflating. He was just as happy as she was, if not more.

"Oh my God, bae. My dreams are coming true before my eyes."

Hot tears stung her eyes and flooded down her cheeks. She smacked her hands over the lower half of her face, taking deep breaths. She shut her eyelids briefly, and her form slightly shook.

"Babe, tell me this isn't a dream, please."

Pain stepped closer to her and hugged her to his hefty frame. Over his shoulder, he said, "This isn't a dream, boo. This shit is real, and you made it happen. All of your hard work paid off."

Treasure pulled back from him. Quickly, he darted over to the dresser and grabbed his black bandana, dabbing the wetness from her cheeks away.

"I couldn't have done this without you," she spoke sincerely, looking him in his eyes.

"You staying up all night with me at the studio, bringing me food, encouraging me to keep going when all of those *other labels were slamming doors in my face. Thank you, babe. Thank you for being the man that I want and need in my life,"* she said, holding his hands in her own.

"Thank you for being the woman that I want and need in mine."

He held her gaze, sweeping loose strands of hair from out of her face and then kissing her slow and sensually.

"I almost forgot."

He snapped his fingers and ran over to his dresser, picking up a yellow notepad. Having picked this up, he grabbed the guitar that she'd purchased him that night they ate at McDonald's. Treasure looked on as he studied the words on the notepad, whispering them to himself. Finally, he tossed the notepad onto the dresser and told his lady to have a seat on the bed. She did, Indian style. While she waited, Pain placed a stool before the bed and sat upon it, resting the guitar on his lap. He cleared his throat with a fist to his mouth, shut his eyelids briefly, and took a deep breath.

That evening, Pain sung the most beautiful song to Treasure. She had always thought that he had an amazing singing voice and that he could have been one of the greatest singers of their time, if only he would have gone a different route than the one he had chosen. Then again, if he would have taken that path, they may have never been together, and she'd rather have him how he was now, than risk not having him at all.

"Ahhhh, fuck!"

Pain's back flew up from off of the bed, and he grabbed his chest. Lines formed across the beginning of his nose, and he squared his jaws. He looked down and repeatedly touched his chest, looking at his palm for signs of blood. When he didn't find any, he dashed to the bathroom and flipped of the light switch. Standing in the medicine cabinet's mirror, he examined himself for any wounds, but he couldn't find any. He thought he was going crazy, because he felt like he was getting stabbed by invisible swords, but there wasn't a slither of blood in sight.

"What the fuck? Am I losing my mind?"

Pain held either side of the porcelain sink and leaned forward, looking into the windows of his soul... his eyes. He wondered what was going on inside of his head that would have him thinking that he was getting stabbed by some mothafucking swords. Hearing his cellular ringing inside of his bedroom, Pain walked back inside and picked it up from off of the nightstand. Seeing that it was his sister, he answered it and placed his cell phone to his ear.

"Bro bro, you still up?" Skylar asked. By this time, Pain was lying across the bed.

"Yeah, I'm up. What's up with it?" he frowned, feeling on his chest to see if he was going to come across a wound. Although he was prepared to listen to her, his focus was on the feeling of swords piercing his flesh.

"Guess who I just finished talking to?"

He could hear her smiling over the phone.

"Treasure?"

He placed his hand behind his head and got comfortable.

"Yep. Well, I just finished talking to her, and I know where she's going to be Thursday night."

Pain's lips stretched across his face and formed a smile.

"I'm all ears."

CHAPTER FOURTEEN

Thursday night

Pain played the shadows, watching Treasure step out of her chauffer driven limousine in front of the W hotel. He watched as her bodyguard ushered her through a crowd of fans asking for autographs and the paparazzi who were snapping photographs. Treasure stopped the bodyguard short and signed a few autographs. She signed her John Hancock on six of them before she was being ushered away again by her hired hand. As the songstress was pulled along across the threshold by the bodyguard, his suit jacket flew open. For the brief moment that it flapped in the wind, it exposed the forty-five automatic handgun he had in his holster. From the expression on his face, Pain knew that he was the type of nigga that would shoot first and ask questions last. He had only had words with Keith once, but it was from that brief exchange that he knew that he wasn't one to play with. This was why he brought along the item he'd need to get past him and into the same space as Treasure.

Hotel security kept the fans and paparazzi outside of the establishment doors while Treasure signed in at the front desk. Pain oozed from out of the dark recess of the hotel and watched the superstar vocalist pass the clerk her credit card and sign in. He could tell by the agitated look on her face that she was pissed off that the media had yet again found out where she was staying. She had complained about this to him before, and he'd told her that he believed that someone in her entourage was dropping the media tips for a couple of bucks.

It wasn't long before Keith was grabbing Treasure again and headed for the elevators. He pushed the up button and waited for the elevator to arrive, looking over both of his shoulders. While this was going on, a concierge was pushing a cart covered by a cloth toward the elevator. On top of it was a silver platter with a bubble lid covering it. At that moment, a light bulb came on inside of Pain's head. Throwing his hood over his head, he slithered through the double doors of the hotel. He stuck his hands inside of his Dickie shorts and hurried his Nike Cortez's across the shiny, Italian marble floor. His head was slightly tilted down, and he was glaring up at the concierge as he waited for the next elevator to arrive, tapping his dress shoe on the surface, whistling. He was about to board the one that Keith and Treasure had entered, but Keith wasn't having it. He made his ass stay and wait for the next elevator to come.

Pain glanced at the numbers aligned above the elevator that the concierge was waiting on. The light flashed on each of the numbers above until it arrived on the number of the floor that represented the lobby, number one. The elevator made a ding, and the double doors slid apart. The concierge continued his whistling as he pushed the cart inside of the elevator. Seeing this, Pain speed walked and then jogged toward the doors, having seen them about to shut on him.

The doors were damn near closed when he slithered his black ass inside. The doors shut behind him, and he locked eyes with home boy that was pushing the cart. The dude's whistling came off tune, and he looked at Pain like he was expecting something. It wasn't until the young thug cracked a smile and gave him a nod that he loosened up and went about his whistling, watching the numbers light up above the double doors.

While this nigga was whistling, Pain slipped up behind him and locked his arms around his neck. The mothafucka winced and tried to break free, but quickly found himself falling weak. It wasn't long before the expression vanished from his face, and his arms fell limp beside him, dangling like cooked noodles. Hurriedly, Pain pushed the stop button and stalled the elevator on the floor before the one the concierge was getting off on. Pulling a small can of black spray paint from out of his back pocket, he sprayed the lens of the camera, watching the inside of the elevator. Afterwards, he sat the can down and pulled the weapon that he secured out, lying it on the cart. He stripped himself down to his wife beater and boxer briefs. He then took home boy he'd put to sleep out of his uniform and slipped them on himself.

Once Pain had secured the concierge's wrists and ankles with zip-cuffs, he put a gag over his mouth. Next, he pushed the stop button in and pressed the button of the floor Treasure would be on. He knew for a fact that she always picked the floor before the roof, because she loved the view of the city where ever she stopped on tour. She told him this when they were pillow talking after sex one night. He had never forgotten this. In fact, he never forgot anything he deemed of importance that she told him. Hell, you could say the same for Treasure. They truly were in love with each other.

As Pain waited for the elevator to arrive on the floor that he'd designated, he adjusted the collar of his blazer and cleared his throat with a fist to his mouth. There was a ding, and the elevator's door opened up. Before he stepped out, he pulled the stop button out so the elevator would stall on that very floor. He pushed the cart out and turned to his right. He was just in time to see Keith shutting the door of Treasure's

hotel room. The tall, old school gangsta pulled his cell out of his pocket and got onto whatever social media site. He became so engrossed in what he was doing that he didn't notice Pain until he was almost on top of him. It was right then that he looked alive and put away his cell phone, taking a hostile approach.
"And just where in the fuck do you think you're going?" he asked, scowling.
"Room service."
"Room service? Nigga, we just got here. She ain't order no mothafucking—"
Pain's fist shot to his mouth, and he blew in it, spraying a white substance in Keith's face. The nigga blinked his eyelids rapidly and made a funny face. He saw double and felt light headed, reaching for his nose. Seeing this, Pain saw a window of opportunity and decided to take it. With lightning fast reflexes, he snatched the retractable baton from off the cart where he had it hidden and struck the pressure points on his intended target. This caused him to grimace and move like he was pop-lock dancing. Once that fool doubled over from a stomach shot, Pain struck him across the back of his head, and he fell over on top of the cart, knocked out cold. Hurriedly, Pain pushed him back to the elevator that he'd left not long ago. It was here that he put a gag in his mouth and placed him in zip-cuffs like he did the concierge. Afterwards, he wiped his hands off on his suit jacket's coat tail and retracted the baton, concealing it. He then left the elevator, the double doors shutting behind him. He made his way down the corridor until he met the room that Treasure was staying in.
****
Knock! Knock! Knock!

A frowning Treasure whipped around to the door, wondering who it could be. Slipping her blouse back on, she headed toward the door, ass cheeks jiggling with every step that she took.

"Who is it?" Treasure called out as she approached her hotel room's door.

"Room service, Ms. Gold," a voice came from the opposite side of the door.

"Room service?" she frowned further.

"I didn't order any room service."

"I know. It's champagne... compliments of the hotel."

Treasure stood at the door with her arms folded across her bosom, tapping her bare foot as she thought on it. If there was one thing that she loved, it was a good bottle of champagne. Being famous, she'd gotten lots and lots of free shit, and most of it was stuff that she had no use for. It was rare that she got anything that she actually wanted, so champagne was right up here alley.

"Champagne, huh? What kind?"

She tapped her finger on her elbow as she continued to tap her foot on the surface.

"It's Moet, Ms. Gold," he responded.

"Moet? Okay, I fucks with that. Lemme get descent."

Treasure slipped the garments back on that she'd taken off when she first got inside of the room. She unlocked and unchained the door. Pulling it open, she found a concierge in a burgundy blazer and black tie. His face was hidden by the shadows of the hallway which was dimly lit.

"How're you doing tonight, Ms. Gold?" he greeted her.

"I'm fine. Thank you, and yourself?" she asked, holding open the door for him to enter. Once he crossed the threshold inside of her room, she shut the door behind him. She handed him a one-hundred-dollar bill, and when she went to pull the bottle of Moet from out of a bucket of ice, he grabbed her by her wrist. Her brows furrowed, and her accusing eyes shot to him. She balled her hand into a fist and was about to fire on his ass until he stuck his face into the little light that the room provided. It was then that his identity was clear to her.

"Pain?" she uttered his name, her brows furrowing further. Right then, he released her wrist.

"How did you get in?"

"I have my ways," he capped with that arrogant smile that she'd known him for. Instantly, her face balled up in anger, remembering that he'd slept with her cousin, Fiona. She switched her weight to the other foot and placed her hands on her hips, angling her head and narrowing her eyelids.

"What're you doing here?" Treasure asked, tapping her foot heatedly. This wiped the smile right off of his face. He glanced down and licked his lips before responding.

"Baby, I came back for you…for love."

"For love?" she scowled and stepped in his face.

"Love should have kept my cousin from sucking yo' dick!" she jabbed him in the forehead with her finger.

"Baby, I—"

"Don't baby me, Trip. Fuck you! Nigga, you ain't shit!"

"What chu won't me to say, boo? A nigga fucked up! A mothafucka apologize," he spoke sincerely. Tears accumulated in her eyes. They took on a glassy effect.

"I lost you. Baby, I lost you, and ever since, I been out here fucked up. I can't eat. I can't sleep. I can't do anything but think about you."

"Why? Why, Trip? Tell me why you chose to fuck with my family when there's like a trillion other bitches in the world? That's what I wanna know!"

She folded her arms across her chest and tapped her foot heatedly, faster this time. Tears slowly manifested in her eyes. Pain hung his head, and his shoulders slumped, arms falling limp at his sides. He didn't know how to answer her question, because truthfully, he didn't know the reason behind him fucking around with her cousin that night. He was lonely, and he was horny, but there wasn't any way that he could tell her that. It would only make things worse.

"You hear me talking to you? Huh?"

Pain didn't answer. He just stood there with his head hung in defeat.

"You fucking, bastard!"

Smack!

Her hand went across his face so fast that it was a blur. When he lifted his head and looked in her eyes, he poked his tongue around inside of his mouth. She could see the blood that had gathered inside of his grill from her assault.

"I deserve that."

He looked her square in the eyes.

"You fucking right you do!"

Smack! Smack! Smack! Smack! Her hand came like rapid gunfire, back to back.

"You fucking asshole!"

Smack! Smack! Smack!

She went from smacking him to punching him. Pain threw up his arms to block her onslaught of punches and moved toward her, holding his head down. Grabbing her by her wrists, he pinned her against the wall and pressed his body against hers, placing his leg between her legs. She struggled to get free, but her efforts were useless. Suddenly, she stopped trying to fight him, letting her head hang. Her shoulders rocked as teardrops fell from her eyes. Sniffling, she threw her head back up, and he saw all of the turmoil and suffering in them. She was damaged goods all because of him. No man had ever hurt her the way that he had.

"You got the perfect name...Pain, 'cause that's what chu brought me. You hurt me..."

Treasure shut her eyelids and shook her head, tears constantly falling. She peeled her eyelids open and continued.

"You hurt me to the core of my soul. You broke me...you broke me into one-thousand itty bitty pieces," she swore to Pain, staring him directly in his eyes. Tears rolled down his face, seeing how he had hurt the love of his life. When they'd first gotten together, he swore before God that he'd murder anyone or anything that brought harm to her, and here he was, being the reason why she was in an emotional state. If it was possible, he'd kick his own ass, but that wasn't going to happen.

"Fuck the money. All I ever wanted from you was your love. That's it. You could flip burgers for a living for all I cared, just as long as you loved me..." her voice cracked under her raw emotions. She was trying to keep it together, but unfortunately, she was falling apart right before the eyes of her soul mate.

Pain took a deep breath and released her wrists. Hanging his head, he massaged the bridge of his nose and looked up into her face, his own shiny from his crying.

"I know. You don't even have to say it," he spoke truthfully.

"Honestly, I don't know how I'm even able to live with myself. I fucked up big time. I blew a chance at happiness with the most wonderful woman in the world... a woman that niggas out here are dying to be with, and my dumbass ruins the shot. Nice going there, Trip. Now what're you going to do?"

Treasure stared at him sniffling, rubbing her arms up and down as she listened intently.

"Baby," he began, taking her hand into both of his and staring into her eyes.

"All I ask is for one more chance. Just please give me one more chance, and I promise, on my granddaddy's grave, that I'ma do everything within my power to make you feel that our reconciling was the greatest decision you have ever made."

Treasure was wiping her face with the sleeve of her blouse while he was talking. When he was done, she locked eyes with him. They held one another's gaze for what seemed like forever. Pain caressed her hand with the thumbs of his hands. His heart was beating fast and hard, resonating inside of his ears. Although she was focused on him, he could tell that she was thinking. Taking his hand, he swept the loose strands of hair out of her face and brought his curled finger around her face. He licked his lips and kept his eyes on her. His heart was still beating hard, but this time just a little harder. He felt his hands moisten as he held her hands in his palms. His eyes moved down and focused on her neck. She swallowed, and her throat rolled up and down. She held her eyelids shut briefly and then peeled them back open, nodding her head rapidly. Pain sighed with relief and kissed her all over her hand joyously. Words couldn't describe how happy he was to have gotten another a chance. He didn't know why she'd given him another try, but he was going to make damn sure that she never regretted it.

Treasure took a deep breath and said, "Okay… alright, I'm gonna give us another shot, but if you fuck this one up…I'll kill you."

"Okay," he nodded. She cupped his face and looked into his eyes.

"No, you aren't hearing me. If you fuck me over this time, I am going to kill you... literally. I swear upon my mother's grave."

"And I said okay… did you hear me?" he cracked a smile, holding her chin up with his curled finger.

"Uh huh," she nodded. With that, he forced her up against the wall, sucking and biting on her neck, trying to give her a hickey. She weakly pleaded for him to stop, but he didn't listen. Nah, he tended to his business. He tore her blouse open and exposed her succulent breast, tracing her areolas with his warm wet tongue, then mashing her tits together and sucking on her nipples at the same time, drawing sensual moans from her. Her head was pressed back against the wall, and she was gripping his head like it was a crystal ball, and she was about to tell a nigga his future.

"Mmmm hmmm."

Her eyelids were shut as she licked her lips lustfully. Pain threw her leg over his shoulder and pulled her black thong aside, exposing her shaved pussy. He slid his tongue up and down her slit, causing her to quiver, growing moist between her thighs. Once he saw her clit stiffen, he flickered his tongue back and forth across it until it hardened. Right after, he sucked on it gently at first, and then a little harder. She squirmed and cried out his name.

"Pain…Oh, my God, Pain. Eat this pussy, daddy. Eat cho mothafucking pussy! Oooooooh."

She wrapped her other leg around his shoulder, and he lifted her up the wall, devouring her. There were sloshing noises as he feasted upon her with his eyelids shut, her natural juices wetting the lower half of his face. Treasure jerked twice as she squirted, soaking him up and then expelling the breath that she was holding. Pain slid up her torso and she grabbed him by the face, slithering her tongue inside of his mouth. Eyelids shut, they turned their heads in opposite directions, kissing.

Treasure wiped the spit from the corner of her man's mouth as she stared at the area that she was tending to. Looking back up into his eyes, she told him exactly what she wanted him to do to her.

"Now, scoop me into your arms."

She threw her arms around his shoulders.

"Carry me into the bedroom, and fuck the dog shit outta me," she told him, looking him dead in his eyes and meaning every fucking word of what she just said. With that said, Pain scooped her into his arms and carried her off to the bedroom door. His hands were full, so he couldn't turn the knob. He kicked the lock of the door three times before it flew wide open. He went storming in afterwards, ripping his clothes and Treasure's off and making passionate love to her. They were lying in bed, pillow talking until Keith came knocking at the door. Treasure gave him some money to keep the hotel's staff quiet and gave him the rest of the night off. Afterwards, they took a shower and made love again. When they hopped out of the tub, Pain dried off and got dressed in a wife beater and boxer briefs. He left Treasure inside of the bathroom putting on her underclothes and tending to her hygiene.

When Treasure was done inside of the bathroom, she opened the door and stepped out. On his knee before her was Pain, holding a velvet burgundy ring box. The room was dark, save for the vanilla scented candles scattered throughout it. On the bed were rose pedals to form a big heart. Snoop Dog's "Beautiful" played from the iPod which was sitting on the dock. Hotness stung the R&B singer's eyes, and tears pooled her eyes. She placed her hands over her mouth, and her entire form trembled. Little mama couldn't believe what was happening right then. Something kept telling her that it was all a dream, so she squeezed her eyelids shut several times and peeled them open. Each and every time that she did this, she still found Pain on his knee before her with the velvet box.

"It's not…it's not a dream," Treasure uttered, taking her hands from her mouth. She sniffled as she cast her eyes down at her man, shivering and sniffing every few seconds and trying to keep herself from breaking down again.

"No," Pain shook his head.

"This is not a dream. I am right here, right now… down on my knee, asking you to marry me."

Placing a fist to his mouth, he cleared his throat and proceeded.

"Treasure Latrice Jones, the love of my life, will you make me the happiest man in the universe and marry me?"

"Yes, yes, yes, I'll marry you, Trip."

She jumped up and down excitedly, tears cascading down her face. Pain took her by her hand and outstretched it toward him, sliding a platinum engagement ring upon her finger. It was a beautiful ring with a pink stone at the center and smaller

Canary yellow diamonds on either side of it. Carefully, Pain slid the marvelous ring onto her finger and rose to his bare feet. They kissed lovingly while holding each other in one another's arms. When they broke their embrace, Treasure held her hand out before her and admired her ring. A smile stretched across her face. In love with the ring, but more in love with the man that had given it to her, Treasure hugged her fiancé again. As they stared into one another's eyes, she kissed him on the lips between his talking.

"Now that we're engaged, I'ma need you to do something for me," Pain told her, receiving her kisses.

"Anything, sweetheart," she replied, steadily kissing him.

"Good."

He broke their embrace and walked over to the nightstand, picking up her cell. He tossed the cell phone over to her, and she looked from it to him, wondering what he wanted her to do with it.

"Call that bitch ass nigga, and tell 'em you came back to daddy. Call that hoe ass nigga right now!" he scowled and folded his arms across his chest.

"Alright, but if I'm cutting off my old hoes, then you cutting off yours too. Matter of fact, yo' ass is going first, nigga."

She tossed the cell back.

"My pleasure."

He walked over to the iPod and turned the volume down. Afterwards, he stood there before Treasure, calling up the women he had been fucking with since they'd been broken up. She stood there watching with her arms folded across her chest and tapping her foot impatiently. Five phone calls later,

Pain was tossing the cell back and waiting in the same pose that she was when she was waiting for him to make his calls.

"This nigga not even answering!"

She disconnected the call after getting the voice mail. Pain twisted his lips and angled his head, saying, "Yeah, right. Lemme see the phone."

He took it from her and dialed up Blessyn. The phone rang and rang, but no one answered, so he said fuck it and waited for the voice mail.

"Okay, the voicemail came on. Tell this nigga you cool on him, and you fucking with a real one now… just like that too. Don't try and play me either. You're wifey now, so ain't nan nigga 'pose to come before hubby."

"And none will."

She snatched the cell from him and did just like he said. Right after, she was throwing her arms around his neck, and they were kissing, walking backwards toward the bed. They fell over onto it and started making out. Then that turned into sex.

Treasure played Pain. She actually hung up before she started talking. Now, don't get it fucked up. She was going to sever ties with Blessyn, but she wasn't gon' be as blunt as he would like. Nah, she was just going to give it to him straight with no chaser.

CHAPTER FIFTEEN

Lil' Joe sat back on his couch with a glass stem between his ashy lips. His bony fingers gripped a lighter tightly as the flame of it licked away at the end of it, causing the off white rocks inside to birth a cloud. Taking a moment to wipe his sweaty forehead, he struck the metal ball of his lighter and its flame impregnated the air once again. He sucked on the end of the stem and pulled the intoxicating fog inside of his lungs, filling them. Holding the flame to the glass utensil, he took deeper and shorter pulls, sounding as if he was taking quick breaths. Lil' Joe looked like stir fried shit, and he had been for the last couple of weeks now. His short dread locks were unkempt, and his facial hair was scruffy, looking like shag carpeting. The wife beater he had on was stained yellow at the collar and around the armpits. He was now a walking, talking zombie. That's right. The young nigga was a mothafucking crackhead.

See, Lil' Joe's nerves were shot to shit. It wasn't because he had been there when Epic blew off Manolo's top, but because he knew that with the death of one of the Forty Thieves' people that they were surely going to come looking for him. He believed that they were just waiting so that him and his niggas would put their guard down. Then, they'd strike unexpectedly.

The thoughts inhabiting his head made him more paranoid than a black man in America being pulled over by the police. He couldn't eat, sleep, or allow himself a moment's rest. Death was looming over his head like a black cloud, and he knew that his days on earth were numbered… that at any given time, Manolo's people were going to come kicking down his door to behead his mothafucking ass. Just thinking about this sent chills down Lil' Joe's spine, and he shook uncontrollably for a second, tapping his bare foot impatiently on the hardwood floor as he waited for the narcotics to hit his system. The moment they did, he was in heaven. A smirk spread at the corner of his lips, and he threw his head back, eyelids narrowing into slits. He blew the leftover smoke from out of his nostrils and mouth, enjoying the effects of the crack in his system. It seemed to calm his nerves and bring him tranquility... that was until he heard a voice at his back that startled him.

"'Sup, lil' nigga!"

"Huh?"

Lil' Joe's eyelids snapped open, and he whipped his head around. Standing in the doorway of the kitchen, he saw a silhouette. His eyes veered to the background and found that the backdoor was slightly cracked open.

"Who...who...who is it?" he stammered, hands trembling. His pupils shot to the gun on the coffee table which was sitting beside a few pebbles of crack. He thought about going for it, but something at the back of his mind told him that if he did, then the intruder would definitely twist his cap back. That's when he decided to play it cool until he saw the chance to cease the opportunity to blast at the cock sucka.

"Who...who are you?"

There was silence, and then, he stepped into the light to reveal his identity.

"Epic."

Fear gripped Lil' Joe's heart like a pair of hands. His eyes widened with terror, and he swallowed the ball of nervousness that had formed in his throat when he saw the twin nine-millimeters in both of his fists. His heart pounded inside of his chest, bumping up against his chest bone. He could hear it beating inside of his ears. The thought of going for his gun again came back to mind, but he didn't want to try his hand at a game of chance.

"What...what's up with it, my nigga, Epic?"

He glanced at his hands and saw that they were slightly quivering. Abruptly, they grabbed one another to keep still. Epic's forehead creased with lines, and he angled his head, looking at him oddly.

"Yo, fuck you looking all scared for, bruh?"

He saw that he was looking at the guns in his possession. At that moment, the odd expression vanished from his face. He understood now why his little homie was afraid of him.

"It ain't even that kind of party, dawg. You know them bloods me and Pain gave the business to that night?"

Lil' Joe nodded rapidly.

"Well, there are a couple of them 'bout to hit the house."

Lil' Joe shot to his feet and spat, "Fuck these niggas know where I lay my head, E?"

Epic shrugged and shook his head.

"I don't know. I saw those fools at a light not too far from here. I was 'bout to let 'em get acquainted with the twins, but the cops showed up, so I decided to follow them, and where did they stop at? Yo' mothafucking house. I saw 'em loading up and click clacking them thangs, so I had to come warn you. I would've taken 'em out, but I was out gunned. You feel me?"

"Good looking, my boy."

Lil' Joe snatched his ratchet off of the coffee table and checked the magazine at the bottom of it.

"Where them fools at?"

Epic motioned him over with his gun and said, "Come here. They're out in front of the house. I'ma show you."

Epic slightly held the curtain open so that Lil' Joe could see who was out in front of his house. The little nigga narrowed his eyelids, slightly moving his head from left to right, trying to see who was out there in front of his home.

"I don't see anybody out there?"

He narrowed his eyelids a little more.

"How the fuck you don't see them dudes, man? They're right fucking there."

Using one of his guns, Epic pointed to the men that he saw out front. Lil' Joe looked closer, trying to see the niggas that were coming for his head.

Blowl!

Epic shut his eyelids as specks of blood hit his face. Lil' Joe's right eyeball exploded and left a bloody gaping hole behind. His lifeless body made a thud when it hit the hardwood floor, blood oozing out of his wounded skull. His killer scowled and squared his jaws, watching the blood and brain fragments bubble out of the back of his dome. Although the little nigga was already dead, Epic was still pissed off. Standing over him, he lifted his tool and finished the job.

Blowl! Blowl! Blowl! Blowl! Blowl!

"Ol' weak ass nigga could neva run with a dog of my pedigree!"

Blowl!

He put one more in Lil' Joe's back, stomped him, and took his leave through the backdoor.

Earlier that night, Lil' Joe's conscience had gotten the best of him, and he made a grave mistake of sending a text to Pain, telling him to watch out for Epic. The problem with that was he was so mothafucking high that he ended up sending it to Epic. Dude was in the middle of watching this crackhead get high off the sample of work he'd gotten from this new plug he'd started having dealings with when he received the message. Once he'd gotten the thumbs up on the product from the crackhead, he blessed the fool with a little something something for his time and went to holler at his little nigga.

****

Epic sat slumped down on his couch, eyes hooded and red webbed as he took a fat ass blunt to the head. Smoke wafted all around him as he watched Belly on his flat-screen TV, occasionally leaning forward to dump ashes into an ashtray. His conscience had started to fuck with him after he had killed Lil' Joe, but he quickly shook those remorseful thoughts from his head, reasoning that the little mothafucka got what was coming to him for his betrayal. From the beginning, Epic had known that Lil' Joe wasn't cut like him and Pain, but they allowed him a spot in their circle since he'd grown on them and was willing to do whatever they asked. Over time, the little nigga had become like family to them, but Epic knew that should the time ever come where he had to go that he wouldn't hesitate to put him down.

Knock! Knock! Knock! Knock!

The rapping at the door startled Epic. This was because he was paranoid when he was high. Immediately, he mashed out what was left of his blunt and picked up his nine-millimeter, approaching the door with caution.

"Who is it?" he asked with his back placed up against the side of the door.

"Ya mama, nigga. Open the door!"

He heard Pain from the other side of the door. Epic took a deep breath and seemed to relax a bit, hearing that it was his nigga at the door. Holding his ratchet at his side, he unchained and unlocked the door, pulling it open. Pain crossed the threshold inside of the house, dapping up his right-hand. The men gave their greetings and sat down in their respective seats.

"So what's up, E? What chu wanna holla at me about?" Pain inquired, adjusting the chain he'd stolen back from Shorty on his neck. The piece was shiny as ever, having been recently cleaned. Epic sat up on the couch and responded, "Got us a new plug, my nigga, and the nigga's shit is fire, too."

Pain sat up where he was perched, leaning forward with his hands dangling between his legs.

"Oh, yeah? What cho people talking about?"

"Fifteen a thang as long as we cop thirty at a time," he explained to him.

"It's a couple of hunnit, but if you put up the otha half, we can get it."

"Cool. I got that."

"Let's roll then. I told 'em we would see 'em in like forty-five minutes."

He rose from off the couch. Pain frowned.

"Hell you know I had the paper?"

"'Cause you hate spendin' money… 'less it's gon' get chu some mo'. That's why."

He smiled and said, "You know yo' nigga too well."

"Come on, foolie."

He tucked his banger on him.

"Alright… lemme take a piss, and we can roll."

"Cool. You know where the shitta at."

Epic focused his attention back on the flat screen TV. Pain went on about his business, journeying down the hallway, in route to the bathroom. He was just about to push open the door when he spotted something down the hall and to his left that stole his attention. His brows furrowed, wondering what it was. Peering closer, he saw that it was a slither of golden light coming from somewhere… a door, more than likely. Pain glanced over his shoulder and then crept down the corridor as quietly as he could.

When he reached the source of the light that he'd seen when he was standing beside the bathroom door, he discovered that it was a smaller room, no bigger than a breakfast nook. When he pulled the nook's door open, his eyes grew big, and he gasped in shock. Inside, he found a strange mural dedicated to his demise. There were several portraits of him ranging in different sizes. These portraits surrounded one big portrait. Among all of this was a filthy coffee can of blood, small to large white candles that were burning, a crucifix hanging from off of the big portrait, a necklace made of alligator teeth, chicken feet, and a voodoo doll that was Pain's likeness and had several needles sticking out of it.

"What the fuck?"

His brows furrowed further, and more wrinkles formed around his nose. *That's why I've been feeling like I'm being stabbed through my fucking body by swords*, he thought to himself. He never believed in magic or voodoo, but this proved that they were indeed real.

Pain's eyes rose from the mural to find words written in blood, ranging from small to large in size. There were words like hate, die, Judas, fake, snake, bitch ass nigga, disloyal, dishonorable, etc. The golden flames of the white candles licked the air and illuminated Pain's face. His eyes wandered up the wall, and he found someone's silhouette behind him. He gasped and whipped around, finding the scowling face of Epic. He had his ratchet out by his side and was ready to execute his ass. Pain looked from the gun in his right-hand man's grip to his face again. His eyes were glassy and burning with flames of hatred. His jaws were clenched so tight that they pulsated. Having recognized that his home boy posed a threat to him, Pain's eyebrows arched, and his nose scrunched up. He already knew what time it was, and he was ready to take it there.

"What's this shit about, E?" he asked with hostility.

"Fuck I do to put chu in yo' feelings, nigga? Speak on it."

With that said, a single tear slid down his cheek, and his nostrils flared. Using the fist he held his burner in, he wiped the wetness from his eyes. Sniffling, he went on to speak.

"The fact that you don't even have a clue as to what the fuck this is about hurts my heart just that much more."

"Homie, what are you talking about?"

"You know exactly what the fuck I'm talking about."

"I'm not a mothafucking mind reader. Speak what the fuck is on your mind, or pull the trigger, nigga."

Epic's face balled up, and he angled his head at his right-hand man, looking at him like he'd lost his goddamn mind, talking to him like that when he obviously had the drop on him. He had to respect him though, because he still dropped his nuts and let them hang on him. Old Pain hadn't grown soft over the years. If anything, he had grown harder.

"You left me to rot in juvy, mothafucka. A nigga caught juvenile life behind that shit we did when we were lil' niggas. I sacrificed my freedom so yo' punk ass could keep yours."

"Did I ask you to do that?"

"No. I did it 'cause we were brothas, you ungrateful mothafucka! And what did you do? You left me to die in the fucking system."

"How the hell was I going to come see you? Huh? I was poor and living on the goddamn streets, or have you forgotten? I had to look out for my sister and LJ… the family."

"So fucking what? If there's a will, then there's a way."

"Hold on, hold on."

He mad dogged him with his hands up.

"You up in this bitch about to pop me over some shit that happened thirteen years ago?"

"You mothafuckin' right. I wouldn't be here now havin' to finish this shit if Lil' Joe's hoe ass would have slumped you that night."

This caused Pain to angle his head and look at him funny. He couldn't believe the shit that he had just said to him. He'd actually sent the little homie for his head.

"You sent Lil' Joe to take me out? When?"

Epic went on to tell him that he'd sent the little homie the night he'd came back from the movies with Treasure. At that moment, the night he'd gotten shot played over and over in his head. He could hear the gunshots and feel the fire in his body when the hot bullets ignited his flesh. Suddenly, he involuntarily touched his old wounds. His right eyelid twitched, and his top lip trembled angrily.

"Why you couldn't peel my cap yourself, nigga? Huh? Tell me that?"

"'Cause I still got love for yo' bitch ass, I'm sorry to say."

Tears ran down his face, and he shook his head pitifully. He hated himself for still having an emotional attachment to his best friend.

"I know that if I pop yo' ass that I'll be haunted for the rest of my life by what I did, and that's why I sent Lil' Joe to handle grown man B.I."

"Fuck is Lil' Joe's bitch ass at now?" he glared at him.

"Oh, you ain't gotta worried about our lil' nigga."

Epic went on to inform him of everything that went down and Lil' Joe's involvement in it. The revelation left him stunned, wearing a shocked look on his face. Shutting his eyelids briefly, Pain swallowed his spit and addressed the man that had become a brother to him.

"Alright... tell me this. If you couldn't bring yourself to pop me then, how in the hell do you expect to do it now?"

"Simple, home boy," he pointed his banger at the man he'd grown to love like a brother.

"I'll shut my eyes and pull the trigger."

He squeezed his eyelids shut and made to pull the trigger. In a flash, Pain snatched the Bowie knife off of the small table that held the mural and threw it at Epic. The knife spun around so fast that it looked like a blur in motion. It landed in Epic's bicep as he was pulling the trigger. He hollered out in agony and showcased all of the cavities inside of his mouth, dropping his weapon. Pain was on that ass lightening quick, throwing them mothafucking hands on his dog ass.

Bwap! Crack! Thwap!

Powerful blows to the face whipped Epic's face from left to right, before Pain tackled him into the wall. The impact busted a hole in the wall and caused debris to fall to the floor. Gritting, Epic kneed his homie in the balls and doubled him over, drawing a howl of pain from him. When he went to grab for his aching privates, he kicked him across the head and made him fall. Epic went to stomp him, but he rolled out of the way at the last minute. Angry, his head snapped all around, looking for his gun that he'd dropped when he was assaulted. Spotting it, he ran to grab it, and Pain tripped him up. Home boy went stumbling forward on noodle legs, looking like he was about to fall face first to the floor. He bumped into the wall and saw his ratchet not far from where he was. When Pain saw his bitch ass about to go for it, he snatched up the Bowie knife and rushed him. Forcing him up against the wall by his throat, he gave it a squeeze as he stared into his merciless eyes. He gritted his teeth and drove the blade into his stomach, causing his eyes to bulge inside of his fucking head. Blood oozed out of him and stained Pain's fist, dripping onto the floor.

"Arrrrr," Epic's face twisted in agony, and he scratched at Pain's face. His scratching pulled his homie's skin underneath his fingernails, leaving red streaks behind. Pain whipped his frowning face from left to right, trying to avoid his attack. Veins bulged at Epic's temples, and his face was shiny from sweat. Suddenly, he got a surge of energy from out of nowhere and chopped Pain in the throat. He followed this up with a kick to the mid-section. The impact sent him flying backwards and crashing into the table that held the mural. All of the items along with the burning candles hit the floor, one by one. Some of the candles rolled across the floor while others rolled up against the curtains out in the hallway. Instantly, lines of fire engulfed the curtains and made their way down the corridor, shining its golden light on everything that it came across.

Pain picked himself up from off of the floor, wincing. He was just in time to see Epic pulling out the knife and letting it clasp to the shiny hardwood floor. The crimson stained blade lay on the surface as its former wielder staggered out into the hall, holding his bleeding stomach. Pain staggered out into the hallway and bumped up against the doorway. Looking ahead, he saw Epic staggering toward the staircase. He began moving sluggishly until he eventually collapsed, tumbling down the steps.

Having seen this, Pain ran to the head of the staircase and looked down. He found Epic lying flat out on his stomach, eyes wide open. He was still, and his eyes were staring off at nothing. Pain took a deep breath and hurried down the staircase. Unlocking the door, he pulled it open and glanced back at Epic. He wore the same face he had when he looked down at him from the head of the staircase. Taking a deep breath, he shut the door quietly behind him and made a clean getaway.

****

Pain hopped inside of his Cutlass and slammed the door shut. After firing up the engine, he pulled off, thoughts racing through his brain as he drove through the streets. The light post illuminated on and off of his person as he drove; the occasional car driving past him. It was all nonexistent to him, because he couldn't get over the fact that he had just murdered his best friend. Pain pulled up to a stop light, and his entire form quivered, head hung. He whimpered, and big teardrops fell from his eyes, staining his pants darker than their original color. When he lifted his head up, his eyes were pink and glassy. His cheeks were wet, and his nose was snotty. The thug broke down as soon as the stop light turned green. Throwing his head back, he wailed loud and hard, the thing at the back of his throat shaking.

"It's your fault. It's your goddamn fault, E, man!"

Pain punched up at the ceiling like he had beef with it.

"I didn't want to kill you, my nigga! I swear before God, I didn't, but you brought it to this!"

He grabbed a hold of the steering wheel and pressed his head against, sobbing. His shoulders rocked back and forth as the vehicles behind him blew their horns loudly and with a vengeance. After a while, the cars drove around him and went on their way. A few minutes later, Pain lifted his tear stained face off of the steering wheel and sped off, tires squealing with him bending the corner so fast. Looking back and forth from the windshield to his cell, he looked through his call log until he found the name that he was looking for. He spat something into the receiver and disconnected the call, tossing it into the front passenger seat.

Urrrrrrrk!

Pain brought the hood classic to a stop before his lady's baby mansion. The front door opened, and Treasure stepped out onto her porch. Her man threw open the driver side door and ran toward her, leaving the door ajar. In route to her, he slipped and fell but got back up, running toward her. As soon as he met his queen on the porch, he dropped to his knees and hugged her at the waist, balling like a mothafucka. She rubbed his head and his back, kissing the top of his head, telling him that everything was going to be okay. She didn't bother asking him what was wrong, because she already knew that it wasn't for her to know. If it was, he would have said what it was over the telephone.

"Baby," she called for his attention, causing him to look up at her.

"There's something I've gotta tell you."

"What is it?" he asked from his knees, cheeks slicked wet.

CHAPTER SIXTEEN

A few nights later

"Yo, who dat?" Snaps leaned forth and narrowed his eyelids when he saw a purple Lamborghini Gallardo pull up in the Nickerson Gardens.

"I don't know, but you know the deal. We murk anything purple that slides through here."

Ace pulled a Beretta from the front of his sagging jeans. His man was right behind him, drawing a Tec-9, letting it hang at his side. They pointed them head bussas and were about to Swiss cheese the European whip when the driver side door lifted. The hoodlums were about to get it popping when someone oozed out of the sports car, one red All Star Chuck Taylor Converse at a time. A jeweled hand grasped the door frame, and Blessyn stepped out into view, clad in a red long sleeve T-shirt. He was sporting a red LA fitted cap backwards. Both his ears had square diamond earrings, and he had what looked like a hundred gold chains on, resembling Mr. T. On top of that, he was rocking two gold Presidential Rolex watches on both of his wrists which were on top of his shirt's sleeves. The gangsta rap spitter was stunting harder than a bitch out in them projects.

"Blessyn? Blood, that's you?" Ace inquired.

"Who else, nigga?"

He cracked a smile and closed the door of his expensive ride. His homies tucked their burners as he jogged across the street, slapping hands with them.

"What chu been up to? I ain't seen you in the hood in eons," Ace asked. He and Snaps were taking a good look at their old friend. He was flamed up and rocking heavy jewels, looking like a straight up rapper, live and in the flesh. That he was. He always told them that he was going to get it popping, and they'd be damned if he didn't. They'd run the streets since they were pups, and when his career took off, he promised to come back and get them which was the reason why he was there now.

"Runnin' up that check. Man, I just came off of tour," he explained to them.

"Thought I'd come back and bless my niggas."

"What chu mean, Blood?" Snaps lifted an eyebrow.

"I came back to get you two niggas like I promised I would."

"You bullshitting, dog. Don't be playing," Ace told him, looking dead serious.

"That's on the Blood, B."

He matched his nigga's serious look, banging the B to his chest.

"I could always use some security, and I thought... why not my niggas, ya feel me?"

"Sho' nuff," Snaps nodded. With that said, Blessyn took two chains each off his neck and looped them over his homies' necks. He then took off a Rolex and slid them on their wrists. Next, he dipped inside of his pocket and pulled out four thousand dollars, giving them two grand a piece. They both thanked him and slapped hands, embracing their longtime friend.

"Good looking out, my nigga, Bless," Snaps told him.

"Ain't a thang, S. Y'all been my niggas since free lunch days. Plus, I owe u that. I keep my word."

"True dat," he nodded.

"Y'all niggas ain't got no choke though?"

He hit an imaginary blunt.

"Hell yeah."

Snaps pulled a half smoked bleezy from behind his ear, cupping his hand around it as he fired it up, blowing smoke. He passed the blunt to his main man, and he took flight on it, eyes narrowing as he sucked on the end of it.

"This shit off the hook."

He took the bleezy out of his mouth and looked at it as if he couldn't believe how fire it was.

"You got some mo of this shit? If so, I'm tryna buy a pound off you."

"Fa sho'," Snaps nodded.

"I got that. Just remind me before you raise up."

"No prob," he responded, holding smoke in his lungs.

"Who this?" Ace went under his shirt again, seeing a bubble eyed Lexus pull up in the projects.

"I know that ain't who I think it is."

Blessyn snaked his neck as he tried to identify the car.

"Who?" Ace's head snapped in his direction.

"Yeah, that's my lil' bitch I be fucking with. What the hell she doing over here?"

"She looks like the singer broad… what's her face?" Snaps snapped his fingers, trying to recall the young lady that had just hopped out of the luxury vehicle.

"Treasure Gold," Ace told him, eyes locked on her as she approached.

"That is her. Y'all take it to the store and get us some drank," Blessyn said as he went to reach inside of his pocket, but Ace stopped him.

"Nah, I got it. We'll be right back. Come on, Snaps," Ace motioned for his man to follow him. Together, the hoodlums made their way out of The Bricks, eyes lingering on Treasure as they went along. The songstress gave them a smile, and they sent some back before hurrying along on their liquor store run.

"Heeeey!"

She greeted Blessyn as she stepped upon the curb.

"'Sup with it? Long time no see."

He blew out smoke and dropped the roach end of the blunt on the ground, mashing it out underneath his Chuck.

"Yeah, I know. I needed the time off," she spoke of her taking time off from recording to go back home to East Oakland. The life of a multiplatinum singer had become stressful to her, and she needed a break from it all, so she took it back home to be around the people that loved her the most.

"You couldn't pick up the phone?"

"Sorry about that. I was just try'na get my head together. This life we live is hectic, you know?"

"Shiiiiit, who you telling?"

He spoke the truth. He was having trouble adjusting to stardom as well.

"I gotta tell you something," she said nervously as she looked down at her fidgeting fingers.

"Oh yeah? What's on ya mind?" he rubbed his jeweled hands together.

"I can't do this anymore."

"What chu mean?" his brows furrowed.

"Us."

"Why?"

He folded his arms across his chest and angled his head.

"Trip and I are getting back together."

"Fuck you mean?"

"Listen, don't go acting brand new on me now! I told you that if Trip ever got his shit together that I was going back to him!"

Treasure's face twisted as she wagged a manicured nail in his face.

"You know what? I'm done here."

She turned to walk away, but he grabbed her by her arm and spun her around.

"Look me in my eyes and tell me that you don't love me anymore."

Blessyn locked eyes with her, daring her to deny what he assumed she felt. She hung her head and took a deep breath, looking back up into his eyes.

"I got love for you, but I love my man. Besides, I'm pregnant."

He smacked his lips and twisted them, looking at her side eyed and waving her off like *get the fuck out of here with that bullshit.*

"Pleeeease… come again with that weak ass crap. I know you not carrying that bum ass nigga's seed."

With that said, she unzipped her jacket and revealed her round belly. When he saw it, his eyes misted, and his lips peeled apart in shock. He couldn't believe his eyes, so he had to touch it, pushing on it gently.

"See," she smirked, looking down at his hand poking her stomach and then up at him, seeing the hurt and water in his eyes.

"How many months?"

"Four."

Hearing that, he hung his head and massaged his nose, taking deep breaths trying to sustain his anger. He was more so hurt than anything. In her, he had found the greatest love imaginable, and she was being ripped out of his life just like he had feared. Although she had told him that there was a possibility that she could get back with her fiancé, he'd never worried about it. He thought that they were officially done, but boy was he sadly mistaken. They had agreed to have a no strings attached relationship… meaning they could both see whomever they wanted without having to worry about the other catching feelings or interfering. She didn't want to go along with it, but he convinced her to.

See, Blessyn was the hottest rapper out then, and groupies were lining up, willing to do any and everything he wanted sexually, so he felt this was the perfect idea. He was regretting it now though. It had cost him what he believed was his future wife. *Damn, right under my nose though? How the fuck was she creeping with homie, and I didn't even notice,* he thought, sighing and shaking his head like it was a goddamn shame. *Then again, how could I see this shit coming though, when I'm out here on my hoe shit, runnin' through these skeezas? Four months pregnant... shhhhitttt.* He took his hand from her stomach and stood upright, tears dancing at the corners of his eyes. He watched as she zipped her jacket up and wiped the tears from her eyes with a curled finger, sniffling.

"I'm sorry that things turned out this way, but we both agreed to keep this thing of ours open."

She wiped her snotty nose with the sleeve of her jacket.

"I'm sorry, Treasure. I know what we agreed upon back then, but I can't let chu go through with this. Ahhh!"

He sniffled and thumbed his nose, blinking back his tears. She narrowed her eyelids at him and coiled her head, placing her hands on her hips.

"What?"

"I can't let chu go. I can't do it, boo."

"Shhhh!"

She looked down, blowing hot air from her mouth and kicking a pebble on the ground. She looked back up at him, eyes bleeding seriousness.

"Blessyn, I'm begging you... please don't make this harder than it already is. Just let me go."

"Nah, nah, nah."

He looked down, shaking his head, feeling his ears and neck warming. He was growing hotter by the second. The nigga was on fire.

"You and I gon' stay together. Once my girl, always my girl, you feel me?"

He pulled a three-eighty from the small of his back, letting it hang at his side. He looked up at her, eyes red rimmed and tears sliding down his cheeks.

"Blessyn, please... I'm pregnant," she begged, holding her belly and fearing for the precious life growing inside of her womb.

"You think I give a fuck!" he raged, spittle leaping from off his lips as he grabbed and yanked her into him.

"Fuck that nigga's baby. It ain't mine!"

"Ahhhh!" she hollered, terrified, stumbling, and almost falling from the strength he'd pulled her with.

"This is how it's gon' go," he began, bringing the hand he held the head bussa with around her back. He gripped her throat with his free hand and stared deep into her eyes, madness glinting inside of his own.

"I'ma slide you up to this clinic, and you gon' abort this nigga's baby. Then, we gon' be together. You understand me?"

He gripped her throat tighter and shook her violently, making her long hair jumped up and down. Tears cascaded down her cheeks, and she gagged and coughed. She was looking into his eyes scared and helpless.

"You fuckin' hear me talkin' to you? Huh?"

"Aaah! Yes! Yes! I understand you!" she managed to say through his hold.

"Good."

"Yo, Bless… Five-Oh!" Snaps hollered out as he and Ace trekked up the sidewalk. He spat on the curb and nodded to an approaching police car. Its headlights were off, and it was flashing a light on everything on their side of the street. Blessyn quickly released Treasure and tucked his banger at the small of his back. She gagged and coughed, massaging her throat. When he looked up, the officer in the passenger seat shined a bright florescent light into his face, causing him to wince and hold a hand over his brows.

"What's going on out here?" the police officer asked over the loud speaker, having seen Treasure rubbing her throat and coughing.

"Ain't shit."

"Are you alright?" he questioned the woman. Treasure looked up and nodded.

"Okay, the four of you... beat it now. I don't want to see your face around here anymore, got it?"

"No, problem, officer," Blessyn assured the officer as he gave him a weak smile. Blessyn and his niggas went to leave, but the officer's next order froze them in their tracks.

"Hold on! Don't chu guys have any manners? Ladies first," he said as he looked over to Treasure.

"Thank you so much," she said, making hurried steps across the street toward her car. Once Treasure hopped into her ride and drove off, the officer killed the light. He made sure all eyes were on him before saying, "Watch your black asses!"

With that said, his partner whisked him away in the police cruiser. As soon as the cops were out of his sight, the pleasant smile on his face converted into one of hostility.

"Punk ass mothafuckas."

He spat on the ground just as his niggas came to stand on both sides of him. They all watched the police car drive off until its back red lights disappeared.

"I hate those niggas, man."

Snaps' eyelids narrowed into slits as he twisted the cap off a forty ounce of Olde English malt liquor and took it to the head, guzzling it, his throat rolling up and down his neck as he drank.

"Fuck 'em," Ace spoke his piece before turning to Blessyn, tapping him.

"So, what's up with ol' girl?"

The superstar rapper shook his head sadly.

"Bitch knocked up by this otha nigga. Can you believe it?"

"Damnnn, that broad foul as all hell."

Snaps tried to give his forty to Blessyn, but he waved him off.

"Cold world," Ace replied remorsefully.

"You gotta get even, homie. I know you ain't letting dude slide for that violation… or are you?"

When he didn't say anything, he went on to plant the seeds that would hopefully give birth to violence.

"Awww, man… don't tell me that rap shit done made you soft."

"Hell nah! Fuck I look like?" Blessyn frowned, looking him up and down like he'd lost his mind.

"Okay then, let's find this nigga, and smoke his ass."

He gave him a serious ass expression before turning to Snaps.

"I know you down to make this pussy bleed like it's that time of the month."

"You mothafucking right, I am."

Snaps sat the forty on the ground before him and stood up, lifting his sweatshirt, showcasing the Tec-9 he'd drawn earlier that night when Blessyn rolled up on him and Ace.

"You with it, then we can hit this nigga in the next few days. I just need to get my hands on a G-ride."

"That's what I'm talkin' about."

Blessyn smiled and dapped them up.

CHAPTER SEVENTEEN

Three days later

The sun was shining through the clouds, blessing those below with its warmth. The electric double doors of the hospital slid apart, and an orderly came pushing Epic out in a wheel chair. His eyelids narrowed into slits under the intense rays of the sun, and he raised his hand above his brows, looking up at that fluorescent orb. A smile spread across his face. He was happy to believe alive. With all the blood that he had lost, he thought that he was a goner for sure, but this cat was on his ninth life...

"Arrrrr," Epic's face twisted in agony, and he scratched at Pain's face. His scratching pulled his homie's skin underneath his fingernails, leaving red streaks behind. Pain whipped his frowning face from left to right, trying to avoid his attack. Veins bulged at Epic's temples, and his face was shiny from sweat. Suddenly, he got a surge of energy from out of nowhere and chopped Pain in the throat. He followed this up with a kick to the mid-section. The impact sent him flying backwards and crashing into the table that held the mural. All the items along with the burning candles hit the floor, one by one. Some of the candles rolled across the floor while others rolled up against the curtains out in the hallway. Instantly, lines of fire engulfed the curtains and made their way down the corridor, shining its golden light on everything that it came across.

Pain picked himself up from off the floor, wincing in pain. He was just in time to see Epic pulling out the knife and letting it clasp to the shiny hardwood floor. The crimson stained blade lay on the surface as its former wielder staggered out into the hall, holding his bleeding stomach. Pain staggered out into the hallway and bumped up against the doorway. Looking ahead, he saw Epic struggling to make it toward the staircase. He began moving sluggishly until he eventually collapsed, tumbling down the steps.

Having seen this, Pain ran to the head of the staircase and looked down. He found Epic lying flat out on his back, eyes wide open. He was still, and his eyes were staring off at nothing. Pain took a deep breath and hurried down the staircase. Unlocking the door, he pulled it open and glanced back at Epic. He wore the same face he had when he looked down at him from the head of the staircase. Taking a deep breath, he shut the door quietly behind him and made a clean getaway.

The fire made its way throughout the house, devouring everything that it came across. Its golden illumination shined on Epic's face as he lay still, casting his shadow on the wall. Abruptly, he blinked his eyelids, and his pupils moved. Wincing, he looked down at the crimson stain where he'd gotten stabbed. He touched his wound, and his palm came away with blood. Epic's head snapped all around, seeing the fire swallow any and everything that it came across. It was hot as hell in the house, and his skin was shiny from sweat. He grimaced, feeling the pain in his stomach, looking pale in the face.

Holding his stomach, Epic retreated to the living room where he pulled the telephone off the coffee table by its cord.

It fell to the floor with the receiver landing not far behind. Epic's bloody, shaky hand reached out and grasped the phone, bringing it to his ear. He dialed 9-1-1, and the dispatcher answered immediately. He told them what happened before darkness claimed him, leaving him unconscious on the floor.

Epic had to be the luckiest son of a bitch to have ever been skeeted from a man's nut sack. The bastard was pronounced as a D.O.A., dead on arrival, when he reached the emergency ward. It took three tries, but the hospital staff was able to revive him. Although he was thankful to be alive, he had every intention of making Pain pay dearly for nearly killing him. He knew that he still wouldn't be able to murk him himself, so he'd most definitely have to have someone give Pain the business on his behalf. He made up his mind then and there that he was going to hire a hitman to do the deed.

Epic stared straight ahead, rubbing his hands together mischievously and licking his lips. He couldn't wait until he was all alone so that he could put in a call to the hitman turned crackhead that was indebted to him. He'd have him take care of Pain for him, and then, he'd take care of him once he was done. While some may have thought that this was scandalous, he didn't give a fuck. The way he looked at it, dead men told no tales.

The orderly had just rolled Epic out onto the parking lot grounds when a blue van came to halt a before him. The vehicle's door slid open, and two masked niggas with AK-47s hopped out, terrifying eyes shown through the eye holes of their disguises. When Epic saw this, his hands shot up in the air, and his eyes bulged, lips stuck open. His head whipped from left to right, wondering what the assault rifle wielding men were going to do. The fools turned their weapons on the orderly, and he almost shitted on himself. His eyes were big and moist, and his teeth chattered. Slowly, he backed his ass the fuck up, not wanting to be filled with some hot shit. The masked up niggas snatched up Epic and threw his monkey ass inside of the van. They then climbed inside of the vehicle and slammed the door shut behind them. In a flash, the van was speeding out of the parking lot, tires squealing as they went along.

****

Six Mexican men in ski masks were the cargo on a raggedy blue van with a rusted driver side door. It was hot outside, and the old heap's air conditioner was broken, so beads of sweat had formed on their faces and the parts of them that were exposed. Dedication and determination was written across their faces. Their gloved hands held tight to AK-47s which some of them were double checking the banana clips of. The driver, one of the shortest of the men present, had long hair that spilled out from underneath his mask. You could see some strands of it over his eye through the eye socket of his mask. His AK-47 rested between his legs. One of his hands gripped the steering wheel while the other held a walkie-talkie. His eyes as well as the passengers were focused through the windshield of the vehicle. An old white drop top Malibu was ahead of them, but they were solely focused on the gathering in the front yard of a house. It appeared to be a BBQ going on as people were mingling and moving about with cups and plates of food.

The long haired man in the mask lips spread across his face and curled at their ends, making a sinister smile and showcasing a mouth of beige teeth.

"Why there you are, little doggy," he said, having spotted Pain in the front yard, cooking the meat and shooting the shit with his niggas. He brought the walkie-talkie to his lips and held down the button on the side of it that would allow the person on the opposite end to hear what he had to say.

"Jefe, we made him. He's here."

"Good, Pablo. Take him."

"As you wish," he said as he dropped the walkie-talkie into his lap and barked to his hitters to get ready. With that command given, one of them slid open the door of the van and allowed the golden rays of the sun to shine in on them. They narrowed their eyelids into slits from the intense rays and grimaced, but right after that, they were getting a good grip on their assault rifles. The masked, long haired driver went to smash the gas pedal but froze his foot just above the pedal once he saw the Malibu ahead of him speed up. His eyes widened with surprise, seeing masked gunman emerge from the vehicle's windows with their weapons. He looked from them to the front yard that he and his men's prey was in, and that's when it dawned on him that they both were there to claim the same life.

Blat! Tat! Tat! Tat! Tat! Tat!

Blawk! Blawk! Blawk! Blawk!

Splocka! Splocka! Splocka!

Treasure was in the front yard talking to Skylar about names for the baby while Grief played dominoes on the porch with the rest of the old heads. Trip was manning the grill and chopping it up with his home boys when he heard tires screeching as an old white drop Malibu bent the corner. The first thing he noticed was the menacing eyes of the shooter who was wearing a bandana over the lower half of his face. He clutched an Uzi and rode the windowsill of the passenger door. Everything seemed to move in slow motion to Pain.

"Y'all get down!" he shouted a warning to his loved ones, and everyone hit the dirt except for Treasure. She was frozen like a deer in headlights. Through her eyes, she saw the car toting the shooters in color while everything else was in black and white like an old ass TV show. Things were moving in slow motion for her also. All she could hear was her heart beating inside of her ears from it pounding inside of her chest so hard. Treasures eyes zeroed in on the bandana wearing nigga hanging out of the window, pointing the Uzi, about to light some shit up. Below his bandana, she noticed a tattoo in red ink on his neck that read *Money Over Bullshit*.

Oh, my God. That's Blessyn, she thought, eyes bulging and gasping. Her eyes focused in on the next shooter hanging out of the back window, gripping a Tec-9. She noted the gold chain around his neck which held onto a three-fifty-seven Magnum revolver piece. The only nigga she knew that rocked one of those was Blessyn's home boy, Ace. Her eyes left him and paid special attention to the driver of the old-school whip. He had a tattoo going up his arm that read *South Central*. This was Snaps, Blessyn's right-hand man. She couldn't believe they had come to murder her entire family. Treasure wanted to take off running, but her legs wouldn't move. It was like they were frozen stiff. All the poor girl could do was squeeze her eyelids shut and hold her belly.

Please, Lord… somehow, make these bullets miss me and my baby, she prayed, hearing the screams and hollers of her loved ones as bullets flew like they were on Vietnam soil.

"Gahhh!"

"Ahhhh!"

"Arghhh!"

Several of Treasure's friends and relatives went down when hot slugs went through them, misting the air with their blood. In one swift motion, Pain pulled his strap and started dumping on the shooters as he ran for Treasure.

Splocka! Splocka! Splocka!

He squinted his eyelids and gritted as he got busy with that mothafucking tool, trying to flat line the entire car before they could steal the lives of his wife to be and his unborn child.

Blat! Tat! Tat! Tat! Tat! Tat!

Blawk! Blawk! Blawk! Blawk!

Blessyn and Ace were spraying the whole yard, trying to lay everything down moving that wasn't already dead. When the superstar rapper spotted Pain sending heat their way, he and his man focused their weapons on him.

"Yeahhhh, home boy... yo' punk ass should have stayed gone."

Blessyn frowned and clenched his jaws, gripping his machine gun with both gloved hands. Together, he and Ace let loose on Pain, sending hot shit hurling in his direction. He took one in the chest and shoulder which caused him to drop his strap. The young nigga fell on his hands and knees, bleeding and hurting.

"Get up, Pain. Get up! You gotta get to Treas and the baby!"

When he looked up, he saw his pregnant fiancé and the cargo of shooters headed her way. He fought back the burning in his form, scrambling after her as fast as he could. Unbeknownst to him, the shooters weren't after his lady... only him. The closer he got to Treasure, the more bullets flew, and the more they flew, the more he caught, tatting him up. Only God knew how he could keep on moving with that many holes in him, but he was still in motion, determined to save the lives of his family. *I know you hurting, but you gotta keep going, my nigga. You almost there... almost.*

Pain's eyes were hooded, and he was breathing funny. With only five feet between him and his love, he used his last bit of strength to leap into the air. Arms spread wide and legs outstretched, he tackled Treasure to the ground, saving her life but crushing her belly in the process.

Urrrrrrrk!

Blessyn and his crew sped away from the murder scene hastily, the blue van toting the masked men speeding off behind them. Dead bodies littered the lawn while blood and gun smoke lingered in the air.

"Ughhh!" Treasure grimaced when she hit the lawn under the weight of her lover. Blood shot out from between her legs as she lay between her man, screaming for the lives of him and their baby.

"Ahh! Ahhh! Ahhh!" she wailed louder and louder, tears pouring down her cheeks and her head vibrating from all of the screaming. Pain lay upon her long dead. His eyes were rolled to their whites, and his mouth dribbled blood onto her blouse. Grief and the rest of the old heads came running down from the porch with their guns at their sides. When the OG turned his future son in law over, he was no more than bloody flesh occupying a T-shirt and Jeans.

"Jesus, sweet Jesus… look what they done to this boy."

"Damn, son."

Grief shook his head sadly, hating to see the young man in a bad way. His eyes moistened, and tears wanted to fall, but he held onto them. Now wasn't the time to grieve. He'd do that after the repast.

"God Almighty, please."

His forehead creased when he saw all the blood staining his daughter's blouse. He panicked, thinking she'd taken a couple in the drive by.

"Baby girl, were you hit?" he asked, concerned, worriment in his voice.

"No... the baby! Oh, my God, daddy... the baby!" Treasure panicked and screamed, hands trembling.

"I have to get to the hospital."

"Somebody call an ambulance!" Fat Rat yelled out.

"Fuck the ambulance," Grief scooped his only child up into his arms.

"I'll take her myself. Fat Rat, open the backdoor of my truck."

Fat Rat opened the backdoor of the SUV for him and stood aside as he deposited Treasure into the backseat. He slammed the door shut, and when the OG went to cross his path, he grabbed him by the arm.

"What?" Grief frowned.

"What about him?" he nodded to Pain who was laid on the lawn, his riddled body a bloody mess. Keeping his eyes on him, the old school gangsta took a deep breath and said, "There's nothing we can do for the kid. The Lord has 'em now."

He crossed himself in the sign of the crucifix and mouthed *thank you* to the young man that saved the life of his daughter before running around the enormous white truck and climbing in behind the wheel. He sped off with police sirens filling the air.

When the doctor told Treasure she'd lost her baby, she was devastated. She didn't eat, sleep, or bathe for days. All she did was stare out of her bedroom window into the street, hoping that Pain would come walking up with their baby boy in his arms. Her father had convinced her to see a therapist, but once she was in the office, she just sat there like a deaf mute.

Realizing that both her fiancé and their son were dead and weren't coming back, Treasure became overwhelmed with grief and knew that she wouldn't be truly happy until she was reunited with her family. She pulled a forty-four Magnum revolver from a bookshelf full of books, knocking literary works to the floor in the process. Treasure dropped down to her knees and checked the chamber of her revolver. It was fully loaded. As tears ran down her face, she slid the pistol in between her lips and into her mouth. Applying pressure to the trigger, she caught something in the corner of her eye. She looked and found The Holy Bible opened to a page… Exodus 21:24… Eye for an eye, tooth for a tooth, hand for hand, and foot for foot.

Seeing this as a sign, she dropped her weapon and crawled over to the Holy book. She picked up the thick brown book and held it to her person, reciting the passage to herself. As she continued to say this repeatedly, she wiped away her tears and sniffed snot back. Treasure allowed these powerful words to soak into her mental and gave them her own meaning. To her, they meant that she should seek revenge against those that had murdered her fiancé and son. Suddenly, she closed her eyes and flashes of white exploded inside of her brain. Right there on the spot, she relived the worse day of her life. She saw the tattoos of the shooters and remembered the chain hanging from one of their necks.

CHAPTER EIGHTEEN

The past few days had been hard for Grief. His daughter was an emotional wreck, having lost her fiancé and unborn child. He tried his best to console her, but his efforts did little to help. She had gotten so bad off that he was contemplating on having her sent to a psychiatric hospital. This was a big decision that he had to make, so he figured he'd take the time to think it over before he settled on exactly what he wanted to do. In the meantime, he was going to spend the rest of the night toying with the surveillance footage to see if there was any clue to who it was behind the rape and murder of his wife. He'd promised her as he stood over her coffin that he'd kill whomever was responsible for her death, and he'd be damned if he broke that promise.

Grief sat behind the glossy oak wood desk inside of his study, smoking a smoldering cigar. Smoke wafted around him like octopus tentacles. His eyelids narrowed as he peered through the fog that he'd created. His eyes were focused on the screen of his surveillance monitor. At this moment, he was fast forwarding and rewinding footage from the night that someone broke inside of his home, raping and murdering his wife. Fast forwarding the footage once again, he pressed pause and zoomed in on the tattoo on the masked intruder's neck just below his mask. After doing this, he pressed play, and the footage played beat by beat. Seeing something that garnered his interest, he sat up in his executive office chair and mashed out his overgrown cigar inside of an ashtray. As he twisted the cigar back and forth, a black smear appeared. The last of the smoke billowed from out of his nose and his parted lips. He massaged his goatee as he played the footage twice before locking in on the ink on his neck. Grief gasped, seeing what the fading tattoo spelled out... *Bullet Boy.*

"Dirty mothafucka."

Grief slammed his fist upon his desk and rattled the ashtray that held what was left of his cigar. Jumping to his loafers, he ran out of his study in a hurry. He knew who it was that murdered his wife in cold blood, and he was going to make him pay...with his life.

****

Epic sat bound to a chair inside of the freezer in a super market that had been shut down some time ago. Dirt smudges and dry blood covered the floor, along with rotten slithers of meat. Epic looked like he had been through the wringer. His left eye was swollen shut, his lips were busted, and the side of his face was lopsided. From his hairline down to his hairy chest, he was slick with sweat and blood. The only thing he wore was jeans which had brown specks from the blood that had dried on them. They'd gotten stained like this from the punches to the face he was given by his abductors. This was how the men that had captured him got down. They started off punching, kicking and stomping him once they'd snatched him inside of the van. Afterwards, they took him inside of the super market's freezer and let him get acquainted with a couple of blunt objects. They'd been beating his ass for the past few days.

Epic's eyelids fluttered, and he moaned from his aching wounds. There wasn't a place on his body that wasn't hurting. For the past few days, he had been getting tortured. He took everything those niggas threw at him, but now, he'd grown exhausted and hoped for a quick death.

Epic dangled from the ceiling, slightly rocking back and forth. The blood from his wounds fell in droplets and splashed on the dried blood on the surface. The two niggas that had snatched him that day in front of the hospital stood before him wearing black leather aprons and yellow dishwashing gloves all splattered with blood and bodily fluids. They wore black sunglasses over their eyes and bandanas over the lower halves of their faces. Both men held baseball bats which had smears of blood on them. Their hard breathing ruffled the bandanas masking the lower halves of their faces and their chests heaved up and down. They'd both just finished beating the dog shit out of Epic.

Sitting on a blue milk crate was a laptop with Desmond on the screen. He had been watching his henchmen lay down their torture game through Skype. Every day for the past five days, his men would come inside of the freezer to torture Epic's mothafucking ass. They did enough to keep him alive just so that they could keep him suffering. All of this was done before Desmond on the laptop up until now.

"Kill him," Desmond told his henchmen. Right after, he disconnected the video chatting session, and the screen went blank.

Epic struggled to get out of his restraints, rocking the raggedy chair back and forth. It squeaked and squealed with all his movements. Looking up, he saw one of the henchmen already on him, baseball bat lifted above his head, ready to bash in his fucking skull. Epic suddenly stopped moving, and his eyes bulged. He kicked off the floor. His chair went hurling backwards, missing the swing of the henchman's baseball bat. Epic's chair slammed into the surface, breaking in parts and loosening the ropes that had bounded him.

Hurriedly, he pulled the ropes from around his form and looked around. Spotting long wood shards that his broken chair produced, he snatched two of them up. Armed with both, he stabbed one into the sneaker of the henchman that had taken a swing at him. He threw his head back howling in great agony as blood oozed out of his sneaker. Seizing the opportunity, Epic lurched forward with a grunt and hatred in his eyes, slamming the wood shard into his neck.

"Raaahhhhhh!"

The henchman's eyelids snapped wide open, and that thing at the back of his throat shook as he screamed bloody murder. Blood sprayed out of his neck in spurts. Seeing the other henchman going for the gun at the small of his back, Epic snatched the banger free from his victim's waistline and brought that mothafucka up, spitting fire.

Poc! Poc! Poc! Poc! Poc!

He cut his ass down, and he went crashing to the surface a bloody mess. Breathing heavily, Epic took the time to take in his handiwork. Satisfied with his enemies' deaths, he searched the last nigga he had killed pockets and recovered the keys to the van. Afterwards, he limped away, holding his side. He pushed his way through the double doors and used the butt of his gun to break the padlock that held the door that lead out into the store's parking lot. Seeing the van that he was transported in, he unlocked the door and climbed in behind the wheel. He slammed the driver side door shut and stuck the key inside of the ignition, turning it. The van kicked twice and smoke fluttered out of the exhaust pipes.

"Aww, come the fuck on!" he scowled and tried the engine again, but the bastard wouldn't turn over. Having grown angry, he pounded the steering wheel with his fists repeatedly until he felt a stabbing pain his ribs. This caused him to grimace and grab his aching side. Right after, he was throwing open the driver side door and jumping out into the parking lot. One hand holding his gun at his side and the other holding his ribs, Epic trekked across the grounds. Looking ahead, he saw the occasional cars passing by. He hoped that one of the drivers would see him and come to his rescue, but he wasn't that lucky. His scandalous ass was on his own.

Epic looked to his left, having made it to the curb. His saw two bright white orbs headed in his direction. There wasn't any doubt in his mind that it was a vehicle approaching. He smiled and showcased the red teeth he'd earned from the beating he took back inside of the freezer. Seeing his salvation gave him his second wind, and he went sprinting out into the street. An Escalade truck came to a screeching halt before him, nearly sending him flying over its hood. The jovial expression he wore quickly vanished when he saw the driver behind the wheel. Grief mad dogged Epic and his top lip twitched uncontrollably. He gripped his vehicle's steering wheel so tight that his knuckles shown white through his flesh.

While the OG went for his banger, Epic was bringing up his and sending some hot shit his way. Grief fell over into the front passenger seat. He missed the slugs that were meant to take his life and whipped out his own ratchet. Easing his head up from where he lay and peering over the wood grain dash, he saw that nigga Epic hauling ass down the street. Determined to see his enemy dead, he grabbed the two extra magazines for his weapon from out of the glove box and hopped out of his car. He left the driver side door wide open, fleeing the scene to avenge his wife's murder.

Grief's lungs were on fire, but he didn't give a fuck. He was going to get that nigga, Epic, if it was the last thing he ever did. Reaching his second wind, he ran harder and faster, gaining on the heels of his prey. His ratchet was at his side while he was in motion, face sweaty and chest jumping. His heart was pumping mad, sounding like a thunder storm inside of his ears. His head was tilted back, and he was huffing and puffing. He moved down the sidewalk, legs looking like blurs.

"Haa! Haa! Haa! Haa!" a shiny faced Epic constantly looked over his shoulder as he hauled ass up the sidewalk, occasionally shoving pedestrians out of his path. Some of the people occupying the sidewalk screamed and got out of the way, seeing the gun in the young man's hand. Epic glanced over his shoulder and pointed his weapon, taking a quick shot that missed its intended target. He went to take another, and his banger clicked empty.

"Fuuuck!"

He tossed the burner aside, and it skidded down the sidewalk, falling off the curb. He shut his eyelids briefly and swallowed the ball of fear that had formed in his throat. Clutching his fists, he ducked and ran as fast as he could to avoid the bullets flying at his back. Once the shooting had ceased, he knew that the OG was taking the time to reload his thang which gave him a moment of time to breathe easy. Looking up, he spotted the police precinct half a block away. He was as tired as a runaway slave, but if he could manage to get through the doors of the department, he'd be okay. There was no way in hell that Grief would run up in the police station and put his ass to sleep. Acknowledging this, he threw his head back and closed the distance between himself and the precinct. Epic cleared the cement steps two at a time, tackling his way through the revolving glass doors. He grimaced when he hit the floor, but quickly turned back over. Hurriedly, he backed up from the door on his hands and the heels of his sneakers. A scared expression was plastered across his face, seeing Grief clearing the cement steps two at a time, ratchet in his hand.

Epic didn't need the time to figure out what the OG's beef was, because he already knew. A couple of years back, Pain had been cut off from Grief's drug supply due to the thug fucking his niece and breaking Treasure's heart. Shit had become rough all over, being that they weren't able to eat and were starting to feel it in their pockets. Convincing himself that they didn't have anything to lose, Epic's nefarious ass broke into Grief's mansion, hoping to find some bricks that he may have stashed. When he didn't find what he had in mind, he took his rage and disappointment out on Rose, the OG's wife, raping and killing her.

How in the fuck did he find out though? How? A million possibilities went through his mind, but when he saw Grief nearing, he'd forgotten them all.

"Hellllllp! Hellllllp!" Epic hollered at the top of his lungs, that thing at the back of his throat shaking and vibrating. Veins formed and disappeared at his temples and neck due to his screaming. The racket he was making drew the attention of several uniformed officers and detectives... even some civilians that came in that night to file reports. Frowns formed on all of their faces, and their heads snapped in the direction that Epic was looking in. In the blink of an eye, Grief came charging through the double doors with hatred in his eyes and murder on his brain. His eyes were locked on the son of a bitch that had violated and murdered his darling Rose. A smile came across a sniveling Epic's face, feeling that he was in a safe zone, seeing as how he was in a building full of cops.

"You ain't gone pop me in here with all of these co—"

Blocka! Blocka! Blocka! Blocka!

That heat opened his bitch ass chest up and killed off the words that came from off of his smart ass lips. Hurriedly, Grief dropped the smoking murder weapon before the law could cut him down. His actions left his audience stunned and upset.

"Fuck the cops, pussy," the OG spat on Epic's corpse and placed his hands on top of his head. A uniformed officer rushed in and quickly cuffed him up, harshly pulling his hands behind his back. Tears cascaded down his face as the cold metal bracelets embraced his wrists. As he was roughly escorted to the back of the station, he threw his head up and looked up at the ceiling. The tears wouldn't stop falling.

"Rest in peace my beautiful black Rose... rest in peace."

Grief shut his eyelids and puckered up his lips, giving his late wife a kiss, having avenged her death.

Hours later...

Treasure stood in the vanity mirror, staring at her reflection. Her tears had dried on her cheeks, leaving white streaks behind. After kissing Pain's bandana and tying it around her forehead, she then looped his famous rope chain with the continent of Africa on it over her head. Next, she ran her fingers through her hair and turned her head from left to right, taking in her appearance. Treasure was going to uphold the oath she took the first time Pain had gotten shot and wear his bandana, or keep it on her somewhere. She would do this in honor of his memory just like she swore.

Treasure's cordless telephone ringing brought her to her right. Seeing California Correctional facility on the screen caused her brows to furrow as she wondered who it could have been banging her line. Curious, she answered and was surprised when the operator presented her with her father's voice. Quickly, she accepted the call and placed the phone to her ear.

"Daddy, what's going on?" she asked, walking over to her bed and sitting down. Grief took a deep breath and told his daughter the truth, leaving her in tears and sobbing. Shutting her eyelids for a second, she sniffled and wiped her face with the back of her fist.

"I want you to know that I am sorry, and I hope you forgive me. I know what I did will forever leave a wedge between us, but I felt within my heart that it had to be done no matter what."

He took the time to gather himself before he ended up breaking down. He couldn't have his baby girl hearing him so weak, because he knew that she'd fall apart. Grief cleared his throat and said, "I love you, baby girl."

Treasure sniffled and calmed herself down as best as she could.

"I...I love you too, daddy."

"Alright, baby. I guess I'll see you soon."

"You most definitely will."

She kissed him through the phone, and he kissed back. Afterwards, she disconnected the call and tossed the telephone aside on the bed. Treasure rose from the bed and approached the vanity mirror, looking at herself. Her eyebrows arched, and her nose scrunched up. Her cheeks were shiny from tears.

"And vengeance is mine said Treasure."

She uncapped her lipstick and wrote down the names of the men that she was going to kill. Right after, she crossed them out.

Scores were about to be settled.

CHAPTER NINETEEN

The next night

The door swung open in the men's room, allowing the loud music of the club to spill inside as an intoxicated Snaps came in with a platinum haired cutie in a fishnet dress that left very little to the imagination. Snaps locked the door behind them and led platinum hair into a stall. He swallowed an X-pill and placed one on platinum hair's tongue. He then unzipped his pants and pulled out his meat, allowing it to hang out of his zipper. He leaned his head back against the wall of the stall, licking his lips and spewing obscenities as platinum hair blessed him with a blowjob that would have put Monica Lewinski to shame.

"Easy, baby... easy," Snaps whispered, feeling platinum hair's teeth graze the shaft of his dick.

"Ouch! Shit! Take it easy with the teeth now. Ssssss, you—"

That was as far as he got before his eyes went wide and glassy. Veins formed in his forehead and neck. His face turned beet red. His lips peeled apart quivering, and he unleashed a blood curdling scream.

"Ahhhhhh!"

He grabbed what was left of his dick, his head shaking like it was about to erupt like a volcano.

"Shut the fuck up!"

Bwap!

Treasure punched him in the jaw, whipping his head to the right and silencing his screams of excruciation. He whimpered like the hoe ass nigga he was as she gripped him around the neck and turned him to face her. Pulling her platinum wig from her head, she looked him dead in the eyes with hatred twinkling in her pupils. The blood from her biting off his dick slicked her chin and dripped on the yellowing piss stained floor.

"Trip sends his love."

She spat blood in his face and held up his flaccid, severed dick for him to see it. Next, she dropped it into the commode where it made a splash, sounding like a turd hitting water. With the deed done, she flushed the toilet like she'd just finished using it. She released his neck and he slid down to the filthy linoleum, squeezing his eyelids shut and holding on to whatever was left of his privates. Around and around his limp meat went in the swirl of water in the bowl until it was sucked into the hole to be lost forever.

Treasure peered down at her lifeless victim with no remorse. She then looked up to the ceiling and smiled victoriously.

"Two more, baby, and you can finally rest in peace."

The rest room door rattling from knocks startled her, and she stepped over her kill's body, unlocking the stall's door.

"Hey, hurry it up in there, man! A nigga gotta piss... shit. I done had four glasses of Henny and Coke," a clubber complained outside of the locked door. Hearing other people pounding at the door along with the impatient man, Treasure opened the small window of the men's rest room and wiggled her way out to salvation.

A week later...

"Ha! Ha! Ha!" Ace breathed huskily as he broke through the woods butt naked, dick and balls swinging as he occasionally glanced over his shoulder to see if the huntress was still on his heels. His forehead glistened with beads of sweat, and he heaved heavily as he made tracks through the trees, scratching up his legs and arms as he went along. Needing a breather, he stopped at a tree and hunched over, trying to catch his breath. The hoots of an owl and the howling of wolves startled him and soon, he was on the move again.

"Haa! Haa! Haa! This bitch is crazy! This bitch is crazy!"

His socked feet smacked against the damp dirt as he flew past the trees, trying to put as much distance between himself and the huntress that was on his heels.

Shhhhhhh! Thoomp!

He got about ten feet before an arrow pierced the back of his skull and came out of his right-eye socket. Ace staggered forward, moving like a reanimated corpse before collapsing to the ground. The horror he experienced was etched across his face.

For a time, there were only the hoots of an owl in the woods, and then came the rustling in the trees. Something was moving within them, disturbing their branches and leaves. A moment later, Treasure emerged from them, stepping forth, one booted foot at a time with a bow gun in tow. She straightened out her skirt and pulled her bra strap back upon her shoulder. She approached Ace cautiously and nudged him with her foot to make sure his black ass was dead before grasping the arrow in his head. With a grunt and two good tugs, she was able to pull the arrow out of his skull. After taking the time to admire her handiwork, she walked back from where she came being swallowed by the trees.

A few months later…

Treasure and Blessyn spent the next couple of months consoling one another after the murders of their loved ones. It was during this time that they both fell in love with one another. The rap star popped the question, and she accepted. They were engaged now and made plans to get married next year. Their relationship now, like their previous one, was kept secret to any and everyone, even their friends and family. They wanted to surprise them all with invitations and airline tickets to Puerto Rico where they planned to get married. Blessyn's eyes were focused on the street as he blew through the stop lights like a speed demon, leaving debris in his wake. The city reflected on the spotless windshield of his purple Lamborghini, the illumination of the light posts lining the curbs shining in on him and Treasure's faces. The R&B diva was perched in the front passenger seat, rubbing the back of his neck and head as she stared at him lovingly.

"I love you, Blessyn," she said as she smiled at him lovingly.

"I love you, too, baby."

Treasure leaned closer and locked lips with him. He turned his head as they kissed hard and sensually, keeping his eyes on the streets. Remembering his 11:00 meeting with Showtime that night at the park, he looked to the clock on the dash. It was 10:45 which gave him fifteen minutes to get there if he wanted to be on time. When Treasure settled back down in her seat, Blessyn switched gears and mashed the gas pedal further.

Vroooooom!

The vehicle looked like a purple blur as it swept through the streets. Its headlights were bright and seemed to be glowing, shining on the paved road as it raced through the avenues.

It was exactly 11:00 when Blessyn pulled up to the park banging Scarface's "Smile" in his European whip.

"I'll be right back, beautiful. Let me just see what this nigga, Show, wants… and then we can breeze, alright?"

He tilted her chin up with a curled finger so that she would be looking into his eyes.

"Alright, baby," she replied before receiving his kiss. Blessyn executed the engine, grabbed his lemon Snapple and hopped out, clad in camouflage fatigues and matching cap, swagged the fuck out. He took a drink of his Snapple as he advanced in Showtime's direction, his iced out cross and Jesus piece swinging from left to right. The lights in the park hit the jewelry and made its diamonds twinkle like the stars in space. He stopped before Showtime and took another drink of his beverage. He screwed the top back on the bottle and slapped hands with the CEO of his label.

"What's up, fam?" he addressed him.

"Who that you got with you?"

He narrowed his eyelids and tried to peer through the windshield of the Lamborghini.

The gangsta rap artist shook his head and said, "Ain't nobody. I'm solo out in these streets."

"You know the streets are talking," Showtime changed subjects, massaging his chin with a jeweled hand.

"And they're saying you're severing ties with Big Willie after this next album."

He cleared his throat with a fist to his mouth.

"Now, I'm not one to take what a few niggas say and run with it, 'cause that ain't never been my style. Nah… I'd rather hear it straight from the horse's mouth."

Blessyn looked him dead in his eyes without so much as blinking.

"Yeah, I plan on making a move," he spoke as if it wasn't a big deal.

"Say what?"

The multimillionaire's forehead wrinkled. He couldn't believe that one of the biggest stars on his label was saying that he was about to cut out on him, especially since he'd given him his big break. Blessyn looked Showtime directly in his eyes, speaking loud and clear.

"After this next joint, I'm out. I took a few meetings with A1 Entertainment, and they're talking about two albums... 1.5 mill. I keep all of my publishing and my masters."

"So, you leave me to find out about it like this... through word of mouth?" Showtime asked hurt, eyes having grown glassy. He looked at the rapper like he was his little brother, so this revelation cut him deeper than any scalpel could.

"I thought me and you were 'posed to be better than this. I thought we were family."

"I was gone tell you, my nigga, but with us celebratin' this new album going double platinum, and seeing how happy you were, I didn't know how to come at chu about it, ya feel me? I was just waiting for the right time for us to sit down and chop it up... real spit," Blessyn lied with a straight face. Truthfully, he got tired of ducking Showtime. The shit made him feel like a bitch, so he decided to go ahead and chop it up with him. Showtime nodded and gripped Blessyn's shoulder, placing his hand on the back of his neck.

"Come here."

He managed a weak smile as he embraced him, tears streaming down his cheeks.

"You broke my heart," he whispered into the rap star's ear and pecked him on the cheek. Right after, he shoved him backwards and walked off. Hearing movement at his back, Blessyn whipped around and met a dark figure. He held his arm over his brow, trying to see the face of who it was standing in the darkness, straining his eyes. Abruptly, the mysterious person pointed something at him that he couldn't make out, but his heart told him that it was a gun. Realizing that his life was in danger, Blessyn's eyes bulged, and he gasped.

"Fuck you doing!" Showtime smacked Keith's arm upward as he pulled the trigger of his forty-five, making the shot go wild.

Poc!

"Fuck you mean what I'm doing, nigga?"

Keith mad dogged his nephew as they stood face to face.

"You try'na kill the mothafucka?" Showtime fumed, clenching his fists, ready to fire on his uncle.

"You said we were coming out here to handle some business."

"Right, and I just did."

Showtime stared him down with a hard face.

"If that nigga doesn't wanna stay down with Big Willie… fine… he can walk. I'm onto the next big thing, feel me?"

"Right, I feel you."

Keith tucked his gun inside of the holster underneath his armpit.

"Don't you ever point a strap at me again, mothafucka!"

Blessyn was scowling with his three-eighty pointed at Keith. His Snapple lay in broken pieces of glass at his boot, soiling the ground. Showtime spun around and hastily approached the rap star with his hands up.

"Whoa! Whoa! Whoa! Easy there, killa... ain't no need for anybody to get murdered," the CEO of Big Willie records reasoned.

"Ain't no need for anybody to get murdered."

Blessyn and Keith's threatening eyes lingered on one another for a time before the three time platinum rapper walked off, burner clutched in his hand.

"I'm outta here."

Showtime and Keith watched as he trekked off, heading back to his Lamborghini.

"You, alright, babe?" Treasure's forehead wrinkled.

"Yeah, I'm good," Blessyn said as he stashed the gun in between the console and the seat.

"You sure, baby?"

She looked him over, feeling over his chest to make sure that he hadn't been shot. He fired up the Lamborghini and sped out of the parking lot, tires squealing.

"Bitch ass nigga, gon' pull his strap out on me."

Blessyn slammed his fist into the steering wheel, occasionally glancing out the side view mirror as he turned into the other lane. He wasn't speaking to anyone in particular... more so, he was just ranting and venting.

"I can't believe this shit! Fuck Blood think... that I just *write* gangsta shit? Mothafucka, I lived it! Don't make me have to show you a rerun out this bitch."

While he went on and on, Treasure just watched him. Seeing her moving around, his head snapped over into her direction as he held a half smoked blunt to his blackened lips.

"What chu doing?" he frowned. When he looked down, he saw her hand grip and squeeze his leg, caressing it to calm the beast in him.

"Nothing, Blessyn. I'm just worried about chu."

"Don't be. Ya man gon' be alright. I can't say the same for yo' boy, Keith, though. That old ass nigga is definitely living on borrowed time."

His eyes darted from the blunt in his mouth to the windshield as he took the time to light it up, blowing clouds of smoke. The screen of Treasure's cell lit up as a text was sent to it, its bright display glowing blue. The R&B singer settled down in her seat and held her cell close to her, responding back. While she was doing this, Blessyn was looking from the windshield to her with curious eyes.

"Who that?" he asked, eyebrows arching.

"Skylar... she's flying out here tomorrow to come see me."

She kept her eyes focused on the screen.

"Oh."

His face softened once he found out that she was only chopping it up with her best friend.

Blessyn mashed the brake pedal at a red light. Hearing laughter coming from Treasure, he looked at her, and she was cackling at a message that was sent.

"What's so funny, big head?"

He tried to look over into her lap to see the message that was sent, but she turned away not wanting him to see.

"Move nosey," she chuckled. Looking up at the front passenger side window's glass, he narrowed his eyes when he saw someone dressed in a black hoodie running up behind him in the reflection. He looked over his shoulder and saw them almost on top of him. He went to grab his three-eighty, but Treasure snatched it before he could. He gasped, realizing that the entire scenario was a setup.

"You fuckin' bitch!"

He lunged for the gun, grabbing its barrel and her wrist. They struggled for control of the weapon. Both of them balling their faces and clenching their jaws.

"This is for my brotha, mothafucka!"

When Blessyn heard that hostile feminine voice at his back, he whipped around and met a face he couldn't make out, because it was in the shade of the hood the person was wearing. The gunman threw the hood from off of his head and revealed their identity. It was Skylar. Her eyelids were rimmed red, and her eyes were pink from crying, cheeks slicked wet from tears of grief. She clutched her P-89 with both hands and took aim.

"My brotha, Trip, wanted you to have these!"

Her eyes bled her mortal hatred as she snarled, licking shot after shot.

Blowl! Blowl! Blowl! Blowl!

The gangsta rapper grimaced as his body absorbed the shots, doing a funny dance in his seat. He killed over and slumped, sliding off to the side. His head leaned up against the driver side door.

Skylar took a cautious scan of the area to make sure no one had seen her lay her murder game down. There wasn't a soul in sight besides a stray dog that was eating something out of a discarded McDonald's bag. She dipped her head down into the driver side window where she found Treasure breathing hard and clutching Blessyn's three-eighty. Her hair was wild, and her clothes were ruffled.

"Treas, are you alright?" she asked in a hushed tone.
"Uhh huh."

She nodded rapidly, taking a hold of the gun with one hand and wiping her sweaty forehead with the back of the other. The sounds of police sirens made them look alive. Their heads darted in every direction, looking to see police cruisers pulling in from every angle. They were rookies when it came to murder, but this had to be done.

"Shit, we've gotta hurry up!"

She tucked her burner at the front of her jeans and reached inside of the driver's window, unlocking the door. She opened the door, and Blessyn fell half way out. His eyes were staring off at nothing, and his mouth was open, clothes soaked with blood. Skylar ran through his pockets taking his money and leaving them inside out. Next, she snatched the chain from around his neck and relieved him of the rest of his jewelry, stuffing it all in her pockets.

"Alright, sis... you know what's next."

She whipped her gun out again. Treasure wiped her fingerprints off of the three-eighty and stashed it underneath the driver seat. She then turned her arm so that it was facing Skylar in full view. Turning her head, she squeezed her eyelids closed and bit down on her fist as hard as she could.

Skylar aimed the banger at her sister from another mother's arm, closing one eye and turning her head slightly.

"Alright, mama... brace yo' self."

A couple of seconds passed and a single shot resonated throughout the night, ringing out like a lone bell.

"Arghhhhhh, fuck!"

Treasure's face morphed with excruciation as she pounded her fist on the dashboard, feeling fire rip through her arm.

Tears bled from her eyes as she looked to the arm of her jean jacket which was expanding with blood from the black hole there.

"Ahhhh, shhhhhiit! Mmmm."

She mashed her lips together hard.

"You, okay?" Skylar asked, concerned, hoping she hadn't hurt her home girl too bad.

"I'll be fine. Just get the hell outta here!"

Her eyes rolled to their whites, and she bit down on her bottom lip hard to fight back the pain.

"Okay, I love you. I'll be at the hospital as soon as I can."

She kissed her palm and blew her a kiss before fleeing into the night. Treasure could hear a car somewhere far off being started and then peeling off. She knew without a doubt that was her girl making her getaway. Looking ahead and seeing a host of police cruisers speeding in her direction, she threw open the door and hopped out. She ran out into the street, jumping up and down, waving her good arm for their attention.

Two days later…

Treasure sat in a wheelchair with her arm in a cast. Showtime pushed her from behind through the double doors of UCLA hospital. On the sides of them were Skylar and Keith.

"Alright, we're almost in the clear now. We've got old boy's funeral tomorrow, so everyone be in their feelings like you're devastated and shit. His family is going to be watching us… his grandmother especially. I'm hearing she already suspects that I had something to do with Blessyn's murder, and she's even spreading the word."

"Fuck that old ass bitch," Keith frowned, spitting off to the side. He looked to Showtime.

"Why didn't chu let me in on this plot of yours anyway?"

"That's what chu tight about?" Showtime asked, pushing the wheelchair through the parking lot.

"Nigga, I didn't let cho trigger happy ass in on what was going down, 'cause I didn't want chu jumping the gun and popping old boy just like you tried to, ya hot head. Shit, I needed it to go down just like it did. This way, Blessyn will die a legend, and this next album will go diamond. Baby girl stands to gain from this, too. An R&B singer with some street cred… her next album is destined to go triple platinum."

"Mrs. Williams really thinks you are the one that brought it to Blessyn?" Treasure looked up at him, seeing under his chin and his nostrils until he peered down at her.

"Hell yeah… lil' does she know, I wasn't even the one that pulled the trigger."

Showtime cut his eyes at Skylar's bubble ass. Lil' mama was looking right in those jeans. He smiled wickedly and poked his gold fangs with the tip of his tongue.

"Anyway, y'all copy that?"

"Yeah," Keith responded under his breath, gnawing on a toothpick.

"Roger that," Treasure answered.

"I got it," Skylar said. This was a secret that they all vowed to take to their graves.

****

"*Bulletproof loveeee. They can't break it. There's no mistaking…bulletproof loveeeee. It can't be faded, baby. We gone make it…*" Treasure Gold crooned the lyrics to one of her most memorable songs to her audience at her sold-out concert in Madison Square Garden. She sang the vocals with so much passion that she had to have experienced a love that strong some time ago. She held her microphone out to the audience for them to finish the lyrics to the song, and they did. The audience was a sea of tear-stained faces of women of different ages and ethnicities. They felt the words of the song. They were heartfelt, thought provoking, and powerful like a sermon from a pastor.

Through tearing eyes, she saw a man dressed in a white blazer and matching T-shirt which he wore a small gold crucifix over. He seemed to be carrying something to his chest and looking in her direction, but she couldn't see his face clearly, because he was a distance away. The closer he came to her, the more his facial features and what he was carrying became visible. The man stopped at the center of the audience, staring at Treasure and wearing a jovial expression across his face. What he was carrying was a baby… a newborn baby wrapped in a white cloth. Treasure smiled and cried. It was Pain and the baby she'd lost that day in the drive by at the BBQ. Pain took the baby's little hand and waved at the R&B diva, saying *hi to mommy, Josiah*. She couldn't hear him, but she could make out the words as he said them. Next, Pain mouthed *we love you, baby. We'll see you when you come home*. Treasure mouthed *I love y'all, too*.

When he blew a kiss at her, she kissed her palm and blew a kiss at him too. The audience thought this was for them so they blew kisses at her. Treasure shut her eyelids briefly and fresh tears jetted down her cheeks. When she peeled them back open, her late fiancé and their baby were gone. Her forehead wrinkled with wonder, and her eyes scanned the audience, but they seemed to have vanished. Realizing that she was at her concert, she continued to perform her song.

"Bulletproof loveeee. They can't break it. There's no mistaking. Bulletproof loveeeee… It can't be faded. Baby, we gone make it…"

THE END

AVAILABLE NOW BY TRANAY ADAMS

The Devil Wears Timbs 1-7

Bury Me A G 1-5

Fear My Gangsta 1-5

The Last of The OGs 1-3

King of Trenches 1-3

The Realest Killaz 1-3

These Scandalous Streets 1-3

A Hood Nigga's Blues

A Gangsta's Empire 1-4

A South-Central Love Affair

Me And My Hittas 1- 6

The Last Real Nigga Alive 1-3

A Hood Nigga's Blues

Bloody Knuckles

Fangeance

COMING SOON BY TRANAY ADAMS

Bloody Knuckles 2

They Made Me An Animal

Dope Land

Tranay Adams

THESE SCANDALOUS STREETS 3

www.ingramcontent.com/pod-product-compliance
Lightning Source LLC
LaVergne TN
LVHW010314070526
838199LV00065B/5555